D1325341

"It's been three years. Too long to just take up where we left off."

"Not so long that I don't remember where you like to be kissed."

Surprise turned to shock when he lowered his head to touch his lips to the sensitive spot beneath her earlobe, slowly sliding them to the hollow of her throat.

His voice vibrated against her skin. "How you like to be kissed."

"Chase, stop." A delicious shiver snaked its way down her body before he lifted his head to stare into her eyes. "We—"

His mouth dropped to hers and, despite part of her brain protesting that a kiss between them just complicated things, her eyes slid closed. The soft warmth of his lips sent her spiralling back to all the times they'd sneaked kisses between patients, celebrating successful outcomes, or held each other in wordless comfort when a patient was lost. To all the times they'd tramped in the mountains and made love anywhere that seemed inviting.

Apparently her hands had their own memories, slipping up his chest to cup the back of his neck, his soft hair tickling her fingers. *He's right.* The vague thought flitted through her head as his wide palm slid between her shoulderblades, pressing her body closer as he deepened the kiss. It had been very, *very* good between them. Until it hadn't.

Dear Reader

When I decided to write a Medical Romance™ set in an exotic place Benin, West Africa, was an easy choice. I could still see the gripping photographs my husband had taken when he worked in a mission hospital there some years ago, and enjoyed hearing his account of the months he was there. It was interesting learning more about Benin and thinking about the kinds of people who dedicate their lives to medical work there and elsewhere.

My story's hero is Dr Chase Bowen, who grew up in mission hospitals and is now dedicated to his patients and to the work he considers his calling. Because he knows from experience that it isn't safe for non-native children in the countries where he works, Chase believes having a family of his own isn't an option. Until Dr Danielle Sheridan returns to his life, bringing with her the son he didn't know he had.

Danielle believed she was doing the best thing for her son, keeping him a secret, since Chase had made it clear he never wanted children. Now that Chase knows, can they make a new relationship work with the challenges of their careers and fears? Chase wants marriage, but Dani isn't convinced. Then a terrifying event challenges them both.

I hope you enjoy reading CHANGED BY HIS SON'S SMILE as much as I enjoyed writing it!

Robin Gianna

CHANGED BY HIS SON'S SMILE

BY
ROBIN GIANNA

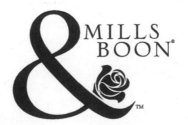

First published in Great Britain 2014
by Mills & Boon, an imprint of Harlequin (UK) Limited,
Large Print edition 2014
Eton House, 18-24 Paradise Road,
Richmond, Surrey, TW9 1SR

© 2014 Robin Gianakopoulos

ISBN: 978 0 263 23887 7

Harlequin (UK) Limited's policy is to use papers that are natural, renewable and recyclable products and made from wood grown in sustainable forests. The logging and manufacturing processes conform to the legal environmental regulations of the country of origin.

Printed and bound in Great Britain
by CPI Antony Rowe, Chippenham, Wiltshire

After completing a degree in journalism, working in the advertising industry, then becoming a stay-at-home mum, **Robin Gianna** had what she calls her midlife awakening. She decided she wanted to write the romance novels she'd loved since her teens, and embarked on that quest by joining RWA, studying the craft, and obsessively reading and writing.

Robin loves pushing her characters to grow until they're ready for their happily-ever-afters. When she's not writing, Robin's life is filled with a happily messy kitchen, a needy garden, a tolerant husband, three great kids, a drooling bulldog and one grouchy Siamese cat.

To learn more about her work, visit her website, www.RobinGianna.com.

**CHANGED BY HIS SON'S SMILE
is Robin Gianna's debut title**

Dedication

To George, my own doctor hero husband.
Thank you for supporting me in my writing dream,
for answering my endless medical questions, and for
putting up with the piles of books and pens and papers
and Post-it® notes that clutter our house.
I love you.

Acknowledgments

For me, it takes a village to write a Medical Romance™!

Many thanks to:

Kevin Hackett, MD and Betsy Hackett, RN, DSN, for
tolerating my frantic phone calls and hugely assisting
me. SO appreciate the awesome scene, Kevin!

My lovely sister-in-law, Trish Connor, MD,
for her great ideas and help.

Critique partner, writer friend, and pediatric emergency
physician Meta Carroll, MD, for double-checking
scenes for accuracy. You're wonderful!

The many writer friends I can't begin to thank enough,
especially Sheri, Natalie, Susan and Margaret. Without
you, my bootstraps might still be laying on the floor.

My agent, Cori Deyoe of 3 Seas Literary Agency,
for her tireless assistance with everything.

CHAPTER ONE

THE POOR WOMAN might not be able to have more babies, but at least she wasn't dead.

Chase Bowen's patient stared at him with worry etched on her face as she slowly awakened from surgery.

He leaned closer, giving her a reassuring smile. "It's okay now. You're going to be fine," Chase said in Fon, the most common language in The Republic of Benin, West Africa. If she didn't understand, he'd try again in French.

She nodded, and the deep, warm gratitude in her gaze filled his chest with an intense gratitude of his own. Times like these strengthened his appreciation for the life he had. He couldn't imagine doing anything else.

Chase understood why, despite their family tragedy, his parents still spent their lives doctoring the neediest of humankind.

"Her vital signs are all normal, Dr. Bowen," the nurse anesthetist said. "Thank God. I've never seen hemoglobin as rock bottom as hers."

"Yeah. Ten more minutes and it probably would've been too late."

He pressed his fingers to her pulse once more and took a deep breath of satisfaction. Ectopic pregnancy from pelvic inflammatory scarring was all too frequent in this part of the world, with polygamy and the diseases that came with that culture being commonplace. He'd feared this was one of the patients who wouldn't make it.

There'd been too many close calls lately, and Chase tried to think what else they could do about that. Their group had an ongoing grass-roots approach, trying to encourage patients to come in before their conditions were critical. But people weren't used to relying on modern medicine to heal them. Not to mention that patients sometimes had to walk miles just to get there.

"Will there be more babies?" the woman whispered.

He couldn't tell if the fear in her voice was because she wanted more children, or because she didn't want to go through such an ordeal again.

"We had to close off the tube that had the baby in it," he said, gentling his voice. "But you still have another tube, so you can probably conceive another baby, if you want one."

Whether she was fertile or not, Chase didn't know. But the children she did have still had their mother. He squeezed her hand and smiled. "Your little ones who came with you looked pretty worried. Soon you'll be strong enough to go home, and they'll be very happy to have their *maman* again."

A smile touched her lips as her eyelids drifted shut. Chase left her in the capable hands of the nurse anesthetist and stripped off his gown to head outside. Moist heat wrapped around him like a soft, cottony glove as he stepped from the air-conditioned cement-block building that made do as the clinic and O.R. for the local arm of Global Physicians Coalition.

Dusk still kept that particular inch of sub-Saharan West Africa bathed in low light at nine-thirty p.m., and he didn't bother to pull his penlight from his pocket. The generators would be turned off soon, and the growl of his stomach reminded him he hadn't eaten a thing since lunch. Finding dinner in the dark was a crap shoot, so a quick trip to the kitchen had to happen before the lights went out.

He strode around the corner of the building and nearly plowed down Trent Dalton.

"Whoa, you off to save another life?" Trent said, stumbling a few steps. "I heard your patient's sister calling you '*mon héros.*' I'm jealous."

"I'm pretty sure you've been called a hero once or twice, deserved or not," Chase said.

"Not by such a pretty young thing. I recall it coming from an elderly man, which didn't stroke my needy ego quite as much."

Chase snorted. "Well, thank the Lord the pregnant sister was my patient instead of yours. Your ego would explode if it got any bigger."

"I'm confident, not egotistical," Trent said, slapping Chase on the back. "Let's see what there is to eat. I've gotta get some food before I have to scrounge for a coconut by the side of the road."

"With any luck, Spud still has something in there for us."

"No chance of that. He left a while ago to pick up the new doc who just arrived from the States."

Spud wasn't even here? Chase's stomach growled louder as he realized the chances of finding anything halfway decent to eat was looking less likely by the minute.

The place would doubtless fall apart without Spud Jones, the go-to guy who cooked, ordered all the supplies, transported everyone everywhere and pretty much ran the place.

"How come I didn't know there was a new doc coming?" Chase said as they walked toward the main building.

"Well, if you weren't wrapped up in your own little world, maybe you'd enjoy more of the gossip around here."

"Do you know who he is?"

"Not a he. A she. A very pretty she, according to Spud," Trent said. "Thank God. As a constant companion, you're not only the wrong gender, you're dull as hell. We're overdue for some new female beauty to spice things up around here."

"We? You mean you," Chase said with a grin. "There's a reason Dr. Trent Dalton is known as the Coalition Casanova."

"Hey, all work and no play makes life all work." His light blue eyes twinkled. "She's coming to finally get electronic clinic records set up on all the kids. I can't wait to offer my suggestions and assistance."

Chase laughed. As they neared the building, the sight of a Land Rover heading their way came into view within a cloud of dust on the road. Chances were good he'd worked with the new doctor before. The Global Physicians Coalition was a fairly small group, and most were great people. Medical workers who saw mission work as a calling, not just an occupation.

The sound of the Land Rover's engine choked to a stop just out of sight in front of the building, and Trent turned to him with a smile of pure mischief. "And here's my latest conquest arriving now. What a lucky lady."

Trent took off towards the front doors and Chase followed more slowly, shaking his head with an exasperated smile. One of these days

Trent's way of charming the pants off women then leaving them flat with a smile and a wave was going to catch up with him. Not that his own record with females was much better.

"*Bon soir*, lovely lady. Welcome to paradise."

Trent's voice drifted across the air, along with Spud's chuckle and a few more words from Trent that Chase didn't catch.

Feminine laughter froze Chase in mid-step. A bubbly, joyous sound so distinctive, so familiar, so rapturous that his breath caught, knowing it couldn't be her. Knowing he shouldn't want it to be her. Knowing that he'd blown it all to hell when he'd last seen her anyway.

Without intent or permission, his feet headed towards the sound and the headlights of the dusty Land Rover. Shadowy figures stood next to it, and he could see Trent taking the new arrival's bulky shoulder bag from her. Spud was obviously introducing the two, with Trent giving her his usual too-familiar embrace.

Chase had to fight the sudden urge to run forward, yank Trent loose, and tell him to keep his hands off.

He hadn't needed to see the curly blonde halo glowing in the twilight to know it was her. To see that beautiful, crazy hair pulled into the messy ponytail that was so right for the woman who owned it. A visual representation of impulsive, exuberant, unforgettable Danielle Sheridan.

Chase stared at her across the short expanse of earth, his heart beating erratically as though he'd suddenly developed atrial fibrillation.

He'd always figured they'd run into one another again someday on some job somewhere in the world. But he hadn't figured on it stopping his heart and shortening his breath. Three years was a long time. Too long to still be affected this way, and he didn't want to think about what that meant.

She was dressed in her usual garb—khaki shorts that showed off her toned legs and a slim-fitting green T-shirt that didn't attempt to hide her slender curves. In the process of positioning another bag on her shoulder, it seemed she felt his gaze and lifted her head. Their eyes met, and the vibrant, iridescent blue of hers shone through the near darkness, stabbing straight into his gut.

Her big smile faded and her expression froze. A look flickered across her face that didn't seem to be just a reflection of what he was feeling. The feeling that it would've been better if they hadn't been stuck working together again. Bringing back memories of hot passion and cold goodbyes.

No, it was more than that. The same shock he felt was accompanied by very obvious dismay. Horror, even. No happy reunion happening here, he guessed. Obviously, the way they'd parted three years ago had not left her with warm and fuzzy feelings toward him. Or even cool and aloof ones.

"Chase! Come meet your new cohort in crime," Spud said.

He moved closer to the car on legs suddenly gone leaden. Dani's heart-shaped face wore an expression of near panic. She bent down to peer into the backseat of the Land Rover then bobbed back up, their eyes meeting again.

"Danielle, this is Dr. Chase Bowen," Spud said as he heaved her duffle. "Chase, Dr. Danielle Sheridan."

"Dani and I have met," Chase said. And wasn't that an absurd understatement? They'd worked together for over a year in Honduras. The same year they'd made love nearly every day. Within warm waterfalls, on green mountain meadows, in sagging bunk beds.

The year Dani had told him she wanted to make it permanent, to have a family with him. For very good reasons, a family couldn't happen for Chase, and he'd told her so. The next day she'd left the compound.

All those intense and mixed-up memories hung in the air between them, strangely intimate despite the presence of Trent and Spud. Suddenly in motion, she surprised him by moving fast, stepping around the hood of the car in a near jog straight towards him, thrusting her hand into his in a brusque, not-very-Dani-like way.

"Chase. It's been a while. How've you been?"

Her polite tone sounded strained, and he'd barely squeezed her soft hand before she yanked it loose.

"Good. I've been good." Maybe not so good. As he stared into the blue of her eyes, he remembered how much he'd missed her when she'd left. More than missed her sunny smile, her sweet face, her beautiful body.

But he'd known it had been best for both of them. If a family was what she wanted, she should marry a guy rooted in the States. No point in connecting herself to a wandering medic who wouldn't have the least idea how to stay within the confines of a white picket fence.

Apparently, though, she hadn't found husband and father material, because here she was in Africa. The woman who had burrowed under his skin like a guinea worm, and he had a bad feeling that her arrival would start that persistent itch all over again.

"Dani," Spud called from across the car, "I'm going to take your duffle to your quarters, then be back to help you get—"

"Great, thanks," Dani interrupted brightly. "I appreciate it."

She turned back to Chase, and he noted the trapped, almost scared look in her eyes. Was the thought of having to work with him again that horrible?

"I thought the GPC website said you were in Senegal," Dani said. "Are you…staying here?"

"No, just stopped in for a little day tour of the area."

The twist of her lips showed she got his sarcasm loud and clear. What, she hoped he was about to grab a cab and head to the next tourist destination? He couldn't remember Dani ever saying dumb things before. In fact, she was one of the smartest pediatricians he'd had the opportunity to work with over the years. One of the smartest docs, period.

"Well. I…" Her voice faded away and she licked her lips. Sexy, full lips he'd loved to kiss. Tempting lips that had been one of the first things he'd noticed about her when they'd first met.

"So-o-o," Trent said, looking at Dani, then Chase, then back at Dani again with raised brows. "Chase and I were about to have a late dinner and a beer. Are you hungry?"

"No, thanks, I had snacks in the car. You two go on and eat, I'm sure you're starved after a long day of clinic and surgeries." She put on a bright and very fake smile. "I'll get the low-down on the routine around here tomorrow. Right now I'm just going to have Spud show me my room and get settled in. Bye."

She walked back to the other side of the Land Rover and then just stood there, hovering, practically willing them to leave. Well, if she wanted to act all weird about the two of them being thrown together again, that was fine by him.

"Come on," he said to Trent as he moved towards the kitchen. While his appetite had somehow evaporated, a beer sounded damned good.

"Mommy!"

The sound of a muffled little voice floated across the sultry air, and Chase again found himself stopping dead. He slowly turned to see Dani leaning into the back of the Land Rover. To watch, stunned, as she pulled a small child out through the open door and perched him on her hip.

Guess he'd been wrong about her finding husband and father material. And pretty damned fast after she'd left.

"Mommy, are we there yet?" The sleepy, sweet-faced boy of about two and a half wrapped his arms around her neck and pressed his cheek to her shoulder. A boy who didn't have blue eyes and crazy, curly blond hair like the woman holding him.

No, he had dark hair that was straight, waving just a bit at the ends. A little over-long, it brushed across eyebrows that framed brown eyes fringed with thick, dark lashes. A boy who looked exactly like the photos Chase's mother had hauled all around the world and propped up in every one of the places they'd lived. Photos of him and his brother when they were toddlers.

Impossible.

But as he stared at the child then slowly lifted his gaze to Dani's, the obvious truth choked off his breath and smacked him like a sledgehammer to the skull. He didn't have to do the math or see the resemblance. The expression in her eyes and on her face told him everything.

He had a son. A child she hadn't bothered to tell him about. A child she had the nerve, the stupidity to take on a medical mission to a developing country. Something he was adamantly against… and for good reason.

"I guess…we need to talk," Dani said, glancing down at the child in her arms. She looked back at Chase with a mix of guilt, frustration and resignation flitting across her face. "But let's…let's do it tomorrow. I'm beat, and I need to get Andrew settled in, get him something to eat."

"Andrew." The name came slowly from his lips. It couldn't be a coincidence that Andrew was his own middle name. Anger began to burn in his gut. Hot, scorching anger that overwhelmed the shock and disbelief that had momentarily paralyzed him. She'd named the boy after him, but hadn't thought it necessary to even let him know the kid existed?

"No, Dani." It took every ounce of self-control to keep his voice fairly even, to not shout out the fury roaring through his blood and pounding in his head. "I'm thinking a conversation is in order right this second. One more damned minute is too long, even though you thought three years wasn't long enough."

"Chase, I—"

"Okay, here's the plan," Trent said, stepping forward and placing his hand on Chase's shoulder. "I'll take Andrew to the kitchen, if he'll let me. Spud and I'll rustle up some food. You two catch up and meet us in the kitchen in a few."

Trent reached for the boy with one of his famously charming smiles. Andrew smiled back but still clung to Dani's neck like a liana vine.

"It's okay, Drew," Dani said in a soothing voice as she stroked the dark hair from the child's forehead. "Dr. Trent is going to get you something yummy to eat, and Mommy will be right there in just a minute."

"Believe it or not, Drew, I bet we can find some ice cream. And I also bet you like candy. The kids we treat here sure do."

The doubtful little frown that had formed a crease between the child's brows lifted. Apparently he had a sweet tooth, as he untwined his arms from Dani and leaned towards Trent.

"And you know what else? It's going to be like a campout in the kitchen, 'coz the lights are going out soon and we'll have lanterns instead. Pretty cool, huh?"

Andrew nodded and grinned, his worries apparently soothed by the sweet adventure Trent promised.

Trent kept talking as he walked away with the child, but Chase no longer listened. He focused entirely on the woman in front of him. The deceiving, lying woman he'd never have dreamed would keep such an important thing a secret from him.

"I want to hear it from your lips. Is Andrew my son?" He knew, *knew* the answer deep in his gut but wanted to hear it just the same.

"Yes." She reached out to rest her palm against his biceps. "Chase, I want you to understand—"

He pushed her hand from his arm. "I understand just fine. I understand that you lied to me. That you thought it would be okay to let him grow up without a father. That you brought *my son* to *Africa*, not caring at all about the risks to him. What is wrong with you that you would do all that?"

The guilt and defensiveness in her posture and expression faded into her own anger, sparking off her in waves.

"You didn't want a family, remember? When I

told you I wanted to marry, for us to have a family together, you said a baby was the last thing you would ever want. So, what, I should have said, 'Gosh, that's unfortunate because I'm pregnant'? The last thing *I* would ever want is for my child to know his father would consider him a huge mistake. So I left."

"*Planning* to have a child is a completely different thing from this and you know it." How could she not have realized he'd always honor his responsibilities? He'd done that every damned day of his life and wasn't about to stop now. "What were you going to do when he was old enough to ask about his father? Did it never occur to you that if his dad wasn't around to be a part of his life, he'd feel that anyway? That he'd think his father didn't love him? Didn't want him?"

"I…I don't know." Her shoulders slumped and she looked at the ground. "I just… I know what it's like to have a father consider you a burden, and I didn't want that for him. I thought I could love him enough for both of us."

The sadness, the pain in her posture stole some of his anger, and he forced himself into a calmer state, to take a mental step back. To try to see it all from her perspective.

He *had* been adamant that children wouldn't, couldn't, fit into his life, ever. He'd learned long ago how dangerous it could be for non-native children in the countries where he worked. Where his parents worked. He couldn't take that risk.

So when she'd proposed marriage and a family, he'd practically laughed. Now, knowing the real situation, he didn't want to remember his cold response that had left no room for conversation or compromise.

No wonder she'd left.

She lifted her gaze to his, her eyes moist. "I'm sorry. I should have told you."

"Yes. You should have told me." He heaved in a deep breath then slowly expelled it. "But I guess I can understand why you didn't."

"So." She gave him a shadow of her usual sunny smile. "We're here. You know. He's still young enough that he won't think anything of being told you're his daddy. My contract here is for eight months, so you'll have a nice amount of time to spend with him."

Did she honestly think he was going to spend a few months with the boy and leave it completely up to her how—and where—his son was raised?

"Yes, I will. Because I accept your marriage proposal."

CHAPTER TWO

"EXCUSE ME?" DANI asked, sure she must have heard wrong.

"Your marriage proposal. I accept."

"My marriage proposal?" Astonished, she searched the deep brown of Chase's eyes for a sign that he was kidding, but the golden flecks in them glinted with determination. "You can't be serious."

"I assure you I've never been more serious."

"We haven't even seen each other for three years!"

"We were good together then. And we have a child who bonds us together now. So I accept your offer of marriage."

The intensely serious expression on his face subdued the nervous laugh that nearly bubbled from her throat. Chase had always been stubborn and tenacious about anything important to him, and that obviously hadn't changed. She tried for a joking tone. "I'm pretty sure a marriage proposal has a statute of limitations. Definitely less than three years. The offer no longer stands."

"Damn it, Dani, I get it that it's been a long time." He raked his hand through his hair. "That maybe it seems like a crazy idea. But you have to admit that all of this is crazy. That we have a child together is…crazy."

"I understand this is a shock, that we have things to figure out." Three years had passed, but she still clearly remembered how shaken she'd been when she'd realized she was pregnant. Chase obviously felt that way now. Maybe even more, since Andrew was now here in the flesh. "But you must know that marriage is an extreme solution."

"Hey, it was your idea to begin with, remember? You've persuaded me." A slight smile tilted his mouth. "Besides, it's not extreme. A child should have two parents. Don't you care about Andrew's well-being?"

Now, there was an insulting question. Why did he think she'd left in the first place? "Lots of children are raised by unmarried parents. He'll know you're his father. We'll work out an agreement so you can spend plenty of time with him. But you and I don't even know each other any more."

Yet, as she said the words, it felt like a lie. She looked at the familiar planes of his ruggedly handsome face and the years since she'd left Honduras faded away, as though they'd never been apart. As though she should just reach for his hand to stroll to the kitchen, fingers entwined. Put together a meal and eat by candlelight as they so often had, sometimes finishing and sometimes finding themselves teasing and laughing and very distracted from all thoughts of food.

A powerful wave of all those memories swept through her with both pain and longing. Memories of what had felt like endless days of perfection and happiness. Both ridiculous and dangerous, because there was good reason why a relationship between them hadn't been made for the long haul.

Perhaps he sensed the jumbled confusion of her emotions as his features softened as he spoke, his lips no longer flattened into a hard line. "I'm the same man you proposed to three years ago."

"Are you?" Apparently his memory of that proposal was different from hers. "Then you're the same man who didn't want kids, ever. Who said your life as a mission doctor was not just what you did but who you were, and children didn't fit into that life. Well, I have a child so you're obviously not the right husband for me."

His expression hardened again, his jaw jutting mulishly. "Except your child is *my* child, which changes things. I'm willing to compromise. To adjust my schedule to be with the two of you in the States part of the year."

"Well, that's big of you. Except I have commitments to work outside the States, too." For a man with amazing empathy for his patients, he could be incredibly dense and self-absorbed. "We should just sit down, look at our schedules for after the eight months I'm here and see if we can often work near enough to one another that you can see Drew when you have time off."

"I will not have my son living with the kinds of dangers Africa and other places expose him to."

"You grew up living all over the world and you turned out just fine." More than fine. From the moment she'd met him she'd known he was different. Compassionate and giving. Funny and irreverent. Book smart and street smart.

The most fascinating man she'd ever known.

The unyielding intensity in his eyes clouded for a moment before he flicked her a look filled with cool determination. "I repeat—my son needs to grow up safe in the States until he's older. Getting married is the most logical course of action. We figure out how to make our medical careers work with you anchored in the U.S. and me working there part of the year. Then we bring him on missions when he's an older teen."

"Well, now you've touched on my heart's desire. A marriage founded on a logical course of action." She laughed in sheer disbelief and to hide the tiny bruising of hurt she should no longer feel. "You've got it all figured out, and you haven't even spent one minute with him. Or with me. So, I repeat—I'm not marrying you."

Frustration and anger narrowed his gaze before he turned and strode a short distance away to stare at the dark outline of the horizon, fisting his hands at his hips, his broad shoulders stiff. In spite of the tension simmering between them, she found herself riveted by the sight of his tall, strong body silhouetted in the twilight. The body she'd always thought looked like it should belong to a star athlete, not a doctor.

She tried to shake off the vivid memories that bombarded her, including how much she'd loved touching all those hard muscles covered in smooth skin. All the memories of how crazy she'd been about him, period. Three light-hearted years ago the differences they now faced hadn't existed. Serious differences in how Andrew should be raised, and she still had no proof that Chase wouldn't be as resentful in his reluctant role as father as her own parent had been.

Now that Chase would be involved in Andrew's life, she had to make sure her son never felt the barbed sting of being unwanted.

Tearing her gaze from his stiff and motionless form, she turned to find Andrew and get him settled in. Chase must have heard her movement as he suddenly spun and strode purposefully towards her.

The fierce intensity in his dark eyes sent an alarm clanging in her brain. What was coming next she didn't know, but her instincts warned her to get ready for it. He closed the inches between them and grasped her waist in his strong hands, tugging her tightly against his hard body.

A squeak of surprise popped from her lips as the breath squeezed from her lungs.

This she was definitely not ready for.

His thick, dark lashes were half-lowered over his brown eyes, and her heart pounded at the way he looked at her. With determined purpose and simmering passion.

"I remember a little about your heart and your desire." His warm breath feathered across her mouth. "I remember how good it was between us. How good it can be again."

She pressed her hands against his firm chest but didn't manage to put an inch between them. Her heart thumped with both alarm and ridiculous excitement. "It's been three years. Too long to just take up where we left off."

"Not so long that I don't remember where you like to be kissed."

Surprise turned to shock when he lowered his head to touch his lips to the sensitive spot beneath her earlobe, slowly sliding them to the hollow of her throat, his voice vibrating against her skin. "How you like to be kissed."

"Chase, stop." A delicious shiver snaked its way down her body before he lifted his head to stare into her eyes. "We—"

His mouth dropped to hers and, despite the part of her brain protesting that a kiss between them just complicated things, her eyes slid closed. The soft warmth of his lips sent her spiraling back to all the times they'd sneaked kisses between patients, celebrating successful outcomes, or held each other in wordless comfort when a patient had been lost. To all the times they'd tramped in the mountains and made love anywhere that had seemed inviting.

Apparently, her hands had their own memories, slipping up his chest to cup the back of his neck, his soft hair tickling her fingers. *He's right.* The vague thought flitted through her head as his wide palm slid between her shoulder blades, pressing her body closer as he deepened the kiss. It had been very, very good between them. Until it hadn't been.

Through her sensual fog the thought helped her remember what a strategic man Chase could be. That this wasn't unchecked, remembered passion but a calculated effort to weaken her resolve, to have her give in to his marriage demand.

She broke the kiss. "This isn't a good idea."

"Yes, it is." His warm mouth caressed her jaw. "I've missed you. I think you've missed me, too."

"Why would I miss being dragged out of bed to do calisthenics at six a.m.?" The words came out annoyingly breathy.

"But you missed being dragged into bed for another kind of exercise."

His mouth again covered hers, sweet and in-sistent and drugging. One hand slipped down her hip and cupped her bottom, pulling her close against his hardened body.

He'd always teased her about how she couldn't resist his touch, his kiss. A pathetically hungry little sound filled her throat as she sank in deeper, doing a very good job proving he'd been right.

But that was before, her sanity whispered.

Yanking her mouth determinedly from his, she dragged in a deep, quivering breath. "This won't work. I know your devious strategies too well."

His lips curved and his dark eyes sparked with liquid gold. "I think you're wrong. I think it's working." He lifted one hand to press his fingers to her throat. "Your pulse is tachycardic and your breath is all choppy. Both clear indications of sexual desire."

"Thanks for the physiology lesson." She shoved hard at his chest to put a few inches between them and felt his own heart pounding beneath her hands. At least she wasn't the only one feeling the heat. "But memories of good sex do not make a relationship. And definitely not a marriage."

"So we make new memories." His big hands cupped her face as his mouth joined hers again, and for a brief moment she just couldn't resist. Softening, yielding to the seductive, soft heat of his kiss, to the feel of his thumbs feathering across her cheekbones, until her brain yelled his words of three years ago. That, despite what he said now, marriage and a family were the last things he ever wanted.

She couldn't let him see the pathetic weakness for him that obviously still lurked inside her. She had to stay strong for Andrew.

The thought gave her the will to pull away completely and shake the thick haze from her brain, ignoring the hot tingle of her lips. "This is not a good idea," she said again, more firmly this time. "Our…relationship…needs to be based on logic, just like you said. None of this to muddy things up."

"You used to like things muddied up."

The teasing half-smile and glint in his eyes made her want to kiss him and wallop him all at the same time. "I need to rescue Trent. You can meet Andrew, but I don't want to tell him about…you…tonight. Let him spend a little time with you first."

"So long as you understand this conversation isn't over."

Conversation? Was that what they'd been having? "I'd forgotten what a prince complex you have, bossing everyone around."

She headed in the direction Trent and Andrew had disappeared, relieved to be back on stable ground without the confusion of his touch, his kiss. Then realized she hadn't a clue where they'd gone. "Where is the kitchen anyway?"

Chase strode forward with the loose, athletic stride she'd always enjoyed. As though he was in no hurry to get where he was going but still covered the ground with remarkable speed.

"This way."

His warm palm pressed her lower back again as he pulled a penlight from his pocket, shining it on the ground in front of her. "Watch your step. Rocks sometimes appear as though they rolled there themselves."

As they walked in the starlight, the whole thing felt surreal. The heat of his hand on her back, the timbre of his voice, the same small, worn penlight illuminating the dusty path. As though the years hadn't passed and they were back in Honduras again, feeling close and connected. She stared fixedly at the uneven path, determined to resist the gravitational pull that was Chase Bowen.

Chase shoved open a door and slipped his arm around her waist, tucking her close to his side as he led her down a short hallway. Quickly, she shook off his touch.

"Stop," she hissed. "Drew needs to get to know you without your hands all over me."

"Sorry. It's so nice to touch you again, I keep forgetting." He raised his palms to the sky, the picture of innocent surrender, and she again had the urge to punch the man who obviously knew all too well how easily he could mess with her equilibrium.

Several camp lights dully lit the room, showing Drew sitting at a high metal table, his legs dangling from a tall stool. The low light didn't hide the melted ice cream covering the child's face from the tip of his nose down, dripping from his chin.

"Hi, Mommy!" He flashed her a wide grin and raised the soggy cone as if in a toast, chocolate oozing between his fingers. "Dis ice cream is good!"

"I can see that." She nearly laughed at the guilty look on Trent's face as Drew began to lap all around the cone, sending rivulets down his arm to his elbow.

"I'll clean him up." Trent waved his hand towards Drew, looking a little helpless. "Didn't see the point of it until he was done."

"Don't worry, making messes is what Drew does best," she said, giving Trent a reassuring smile. "Right, honey?"

"Wight!" Drew shoved his mouth into the cone, and the softened ice cream globbed onto the table. He promptly dropped his face to slurp it straight from the flat metal surface then swirled his tongue, making circles in the melty chocolate.

"Okay, no licking the table." Chase probably thought she'd never taught the boy manners. Hastily, she walked over to lift his wet, sticky chin with her palm. "Finish your cone, then we'll find out where we're sleeping. And you'd better do it quick, 'coz it's about to become all cream without the ice part."

"You know, Drew," Chase said in a jocular tone that sounded a little forced, "when you stick your tongue out like that, you look like a lizard. We have big ones around here. Maybe tomorrow we'll look for one."

Drew's eyes lit and he paused his licking to look up at Chase. "Lizards?"

"Yep. Maybe we'll catch one to keep for a day or two. Find bugs to feed it." Chase moved from the sink with two wet cloths in his hands. His thick shoulder pressed against Dani's as he efficiently wiped the chocolaty table with one cloth then handed it to Trent, whose expression was a comical combination of amusement and disgust.

Chase lifted the other cloth to Drew's mouth, his gaze suddenly riveted on the little boy's face. *Their* baby's face. Still cupping Drew's chin in her hand, Dani stared at Chase. Every emotion crossed his face that she'd long imagined might be there if he knew about his son. Within the shadowy light she imagined that through all those mixed emotions it wasn't horror that shone through but joy. Or was that just wishful thinking?

Her breath caught, remembering how many times in the past two and a half years she'd thought about what this moment might be like. After the miracle of Drew as a newborn and when he'd cried through the night. When he'd first smiled. Crawled. Run.

Her throat closed and she fought back silly tears that stung the backs of her eyes as Chase lifted his gaze to hers, wonder filling his.

The sound of Trent clearing his throat broke the strange spell that seemed to have frozen the moment in time.

"I'm going to head to my room, you three. See you in the a.m.," Trent said, smiling at Drew.

Heat filled Dani's face. "I appreciate you getting him the ice cream. I don't think there's much doubt he enjoyed it."

"Yeah, thanks, Trent." Chase and he exchanged a look and a nod before Trent took off, and Dani could see the two of them were good friends. Something that often happened when working in the GPC community, but not always. Occasionally personalities just didn't mesh and a strictly professional relationship became the best outcome.

Then there were those rare times that an intimate relationship took over your whole world.

"I think this one's done, Lizard-Boy," Chase said, taking what remained of the soggy cone and tossing it in the trash. He took over the clean-up with an efficiency that implied he'd had dozens of children in his life, wiping Drew's hands then pulling Dani's hand from her son's chin, about to take care of his gooey face, too.

The frown on Drew's face as he stared at the stranger washing his face while his mother stood motionless snapped her out of her stupor.

She tugged the cloth from Chase's hand and took over. "I'm not sure if you ate the cone, or the cone ate you," she said lightly. She rinsed it again, along with her own sticky hand, before dabbing at the last spots on Drew's face.

"Dat's enough, Mommy." Drew yanked his head away as she tried for one last swipe of his chin.

Spud poked his head into the kitchen. "Everything's ready, if you are, Dani. Tomorrow Ruth is coming to meet both of you and take care of

Drew while we give you the low-down around here."

"Great. Thanks." She lifted Drew onto her hip and turned to Chase, inhaling a fortifying breath. "We'll see you tomorrow."

"Yes." His gaze lingered on Drew. When he finally looked at Dani, his eyes were hooded and his expression serious. "Tomorrow will be a big day."

Dani awoke to a cool draft, and she realized Drew was in the process of yanking off her bed sheet.

"Hey, you, that's not nice. I'm sleeping."

No way could it be morning already. She pulled the covers back to her chin but Drew tugged harder.

"Get up. I hungry."

She peeled open one eye. From the crack visible between the curtains, it looked like the sun had barely risen above the horizon. "It's too early to be hungry."

"Uh-uh. My tummy monsters are growling."

Even through her sleep-dulled senses Dani had to smile. Drew loved the idea of feeding the "monsters" that growled in his stomach. "What color monster's in there today?"

"Blue. And green. Wif big teeth."

He tugged again. Dani sighed and gave up on the idea of more sleep. Doubtless both their body clocks were off, and no wonder. Sleeping on a plane was something she never managed to do well, but Drew had conked out both on the plane and in the car, and she'd been amazed he'd slept at all once he'd got into bed.

"All right. Let's see what there is to eat."

She threw on some clothes but left Drew in his Spiderman pajamas. It took a minute to remember which door led to the kitchen, and she hesitated in the hallway. Getting it wrong and ending up in someone's bedroom was an embarrassment she didn't need. Cautiously, she cracked open the door, relieved to see a refrigerator instead of a sexy, sleeping Chase Bowen.

"Let's see what your monster wants," she said, pushing the door wide as she nudged Drew inside. To her surprise, Trent was sitting at the table, sipping coffee and reading.

"When I took this job, no one told me the

hours here were dawn to dusk," Dani joked as she plopped Drew onto the same stool he'd sat on the night before.

"Spud's a slave driver, I tell you," Trent said with an exaggerated sigh. "Actually, I just finished up an emergency surgery. Clinic hours don't usually start until nine. Coffee?"

He started to get up, but she waved her hand when she spied the percolator on the counter. "Thanks, I'll grab it myself." Last night, the darkness had obscured most of the kitchen, but this morning showed it to be big and functional, if a bit utilitarian.

"So, do you and Chase share a room?" As soon as the words left her mouth she wondered why in the world she'd asked. She stared into her cup as she poured, heat filling her face at the look of impassive assessment Trent gave her in response.

"No. The medical workers used to stay with families nearby, but they built the sleeping quarters you're in a couple years ago, with small rooms for everyone."

"Oh. Can you tell me where there's oatmeal or something for Drew?"

"Top cupboard on the left. Spud fixes breakfast around eight. Chase runs every morning." He leaned his back against the table and sipped his coffee. "But you probably know that."

She did know. The man was a physical fitness nut. "How long have you worked with Chase?"

"We've worked together in the Philippines and Ghana. Been here a year. Both our commissions are up, but we're hanging around until there are other surgeons here and we get new assignments."

Did that mean Chase might not be here long? A sharp pang of dismay stabbed at her, which was both ridiculous and disturbing. Shouldn't she feel relief instead? It would be so much better for Drew if Chase moved on before the two got too close.

"Mommy, I need food," Drew said, fidgeting on his stool.

Lord, she had to be sure this whole mess didn't distract her from the work she'd come to Africa to do. If she couldn't even get Drew's breakfast going, she was in serious trouble.

In a sign that their new, temporary home was

practically made for her and Drew, two of his favorite foods sat in the cupboard. Dani microwaved the apple-flavored oatmeal and opened a box of raisins.

Trent got up and pulled some construction paper and crayons from a drawer to place them in front of Drew, poking a finger at his pajama top. "While your mom gets your breakfast, how about drawing me a picture of Spiderman climbing a wall?"

Wow, the man sure knew kids, and she wondered what Trent's story was. Just as she was about to ask, he beat her to the questions.

"So, obviously you and Chase go back a while. Where did you meet?"

"Honduras." Back then, her expectations for mission work had been so starry-eyed and naive. And the last thing she'd expected was to meet a hunky, dynamic doctor who'd knocked her socks off. Among other things.

Apparently, Trent expected more than a one-word answer, looking at her speculatively. It was pretty clear he wondered if her arrival was bad for Chase. Her stomach twisted. Who knew if this situation they were in was good or bad for any of them?

"I'd just finished my pediatric residency and wanted to do something important for a while," she said, tucking raisins into the steamy oatmeal to make a smiley face. "Go where kids don't get the kind of medical care we have at home."

She didn't add that she'd stayed months after her contract was up because she hadn't been ready to say goodbye. Knew she'd never be ready. Until she was forced to be.

She slid Drew's artwork aside to make room for his breakfast. He picked the raisins out one at a time and shoved them in his mouth. "He can't see now! I ate his eyes!"

A smile touched Trent's face as he watched Drew dig into his breakfast, but when he turned to Dani, his expression cooled.

"So, why didn't you tell Chase? Frankly, I think that's pretty lame."

She gulped her coffee to swallow the burning ache in her chest that was anger and remorse combined. Who was he to judge her without knowing Chase's attitude? Without knowing she'd had to protect her baby? Without knowing how hard it had been to leave the man she'd fallen crazy in love with?

"Listen, I—"

The kitchen door swung open and the man in question walked in, which immediately sent her pulse hammering at the thought of what lay ahead of them. Telling Drew, and what his reaction would be when he learned Chase was his daddy. What demands Chase might or might not make in being a part of his son's life. How it all could be balanced without Drew getting hurt.

Chase filled the doorway, sweat glistening on his tanned arms and face, spikes of dark hair sticking to his neck. A faded gray T-shirt damply clung to his broad chest, his running shorts exposing his strong calves and thighs. His brows rose as he paused in mid-stride, wiping his forehead with the sleeve of his shirt.

"What is this, a sunrise party? Not used to seeing anyone in here this early."

She tore her gaze from his sexy body to focus on wiping Drew's chin. "Andrew needed food more than he needed sleep. Guess we're not on West Africa time yet."

Chase grabbed a bottle of cold water from the fridge and took a big swig as he leaned his hip against the counter, his attention fixed on Drew. Dani found herself staring as he swallowed. As his tongue licked droplets of water from his lips.

Quickly, she glanced away and swallowed hard herself. Why couldn't she just concentrate on the serious issues that lay between them, instead of wanting to grab him and sip that water from his lips herself?

Toughening up was clearly essential, and she braved another look at him, sternly reminding herself they'd been apart way longer than they'd been together. His demeanor seemed relaxed, but she could sense the undercurrent of tension in the set of his shoulders, the tightness in his jaw. Obviously, he felt as anxious about their upcoming revelation to Drew as she did.

Trent stood. "Think I'll get in a catnap before the clinic opens."

"Don't worry about getting to the clinic at nine.

I can't take how cranky you get when you're tired," Chase said.

"Better than being cranky all the time, like you," Trent said, slapping Chase on the back. "See you all later."

The kitchen seemed to become suffocatingly small as Chase stepped so close to Dani that his shoulder brushed hers. His expression told her clearly that it was showtime, and her pulse rocketed.

Why did she feel so petrified? At least a thousand times since he'd been born, she'd thought about how or if or when she'd tell Drew about his daddy. He was still practically a baby after all. Like she'd said last night, he probably wouldn't think anything of it.

But as she looked at her little boy, the words stuck in her throat. She turned to Chase, and he seemed to sense all the crazy emotions whirling through her. The intensity on his face relaxed, his deep brown eyes softened, and he slipped his arm around her shoulders.

"I promise you it will be okay," he said, dropping a kiss on her forehead. "No. Way better than okay. So stop worrying."

She nodded. No point in telling him she'd been worrying since before Drew had been born, and couldn't just turn it off now. But deep inside she somehow knew that, even though he hadn't wanted a child, Chase would never say and do the hurtful things her own father had.

Chase released her shoulders and pulled two stools on either side of Drew's before propping himself on one and gesturing to Dani to sit on the other. She sank onto the stool and hoped her smile covered up how her stomach churned and her heart pounded.

She wiped the last of his breakfast from Drew's hands and face and slid his bowl aside. "Drew, you know Mommy brought you to Africa so I could work with children here. But I brought you here for another reason, too."

Okay, so that was a total lie, and the twist of Chase's lips showed her he was still ticked about not knowing about Drew. But she was going with it anyway, darn it.

"And that reason is…because…" She gulped

and struggled with the next words. "Dr. Chase here is, um…"

She was making a complete mess of this. Drew looked at her quizzically and she cleared her throat, trying to unstick the words that seemed lodged in there.

Chase made an impatient sound and leaned forward. "What your mom is trying to say is that I'm really happy to finally meet you and be with you because—"

The door to the kitchen swung wide and Spud strode in with hurricane force. "A truck plowed down two kids walking to school. One's pretty beat up. I have them in pre-op now."

Chase straightened and briefly looked conflicted before becoming all business. He stood, downed the last of his water and looked at Drew, then focused on Dani, his expression hardened with frustration. "We'll talk later."

Spud turned to her. "Ruth is on her way to take care of Andrew," he said. "I'll show you the facility and the clinic schedule after he's settled in."

"I want to help with the injured children as soon as she gets here," Dani said. She wasn't about to let the drama with Chase interfere with her reason for being here in the first place, and caring for sick and injured children was a big part of that reason.

Spud inclined his head and left. Chase paused a moment next to Drew and seemed to hesitate before crouching down next to him.

Dani's heart pinched as she saw the usually decisive expression on Chase's face replaced by a peculiar mix of uncertainty, determination and worry.

"Later today, how about you and your mom and I go look for those lizards?"

"'K." Drew beamed at Chase before grabbing his crayons to scribble on his Spiderman artwork.

Chase strode to the door, stopping to give Dani a look that brooked no argument. "Plan on a little trek this afternoon."

CHAPTER THREE

WITH DREW HAPPILY playing under the watchful eye of a gentle local woman, Ruth, Dani hurried to the prep room Spud directed her to.

The room, only about fifteen feet by twenty or so, echoed with the whimpers of a child. The harsh, fluorescent light seemed to bounce off the white cinder-block walls, magnifying the horror of one child's injuries.

Chase was leaning over the boy as he lay on a gurney, speaking soothingly in some language she'd never heard as he focused on the child's leg. She'd almost forgotten how Chase simply radiated strength, calm, and utter competence when caring for his patients. The boy nodded and hiccupped as he took deep breaths, an expression of trust on his face despite the fear and pain etched there.

Dani looked at the boy's leg and nearly showed

her reaction to his injury, but caught herself just in time. Jaggedly broken, the child's femur protruded through the flesh of his thigh. Gravel and twigs and who-knew-what were embedded in the swollen wound. His lower leg was badly scraped and lacerated and full of road debris too, and his forehead had a gash that obviously required suturing.

The other child, at first glance anyway, seemed to have suffered less severe injuries.

She looked to be about eight years old. Her wounds would need suturing, too, and before that a thorough cleaning. A woman, presumably her mother, sat with her, tenderly wiping her scrapes and cuts with damp cotton pads.

"What do you need me to do first?" Dani asked. She'd probably be stitching up the girl but, as bad as the boy's injuries looked, Chase might need her help first.

"Get a peripheral IV going in the boy. His name's Apollo. Give him morphine so I can irrigate and set the leg. Then you can wash out his sister's cuts, scrub with soap and stitch her up.

I have her mom putting a lidocaine-epinephrine cocktail on her to numb the skin."

Dani noted how worried the mother looked, and had to applaud her for her calm and efficient ministrations. A cloth that looked like it might have been the boy's shirt lay soaked with blood on the floor next to her, which, at a guess, she'd used to try to stop the bleeding. The mother's clothes were covered in blood too, and Dani's throat tightened in sympathy. The poor woman had sure been through one terrible morning.

"Where are the IVs kept? And the irrigation and suture kits?" If only she'd had just an hour to get acquainted with the layout of the place. Right now, she felt like the newbie she was, and hated her inadequacy when both patients needed help fast.

"IVs are in the top right cupboard. The key to the drug drawer is in my scrub pocket."

She stepped over to Chase, and he straightened to give her access to his chest pocket. As she slipped her hand inside, feeling his hard pectoral through the fabric, their eyes met. The moment took her rushing back to Honduras, to all the times just like these, as though they had been yesterday instead of three years ago. To all the memories of working together as a team. To all the times he'd proved what an accomplished surgeon he was.

Heart fluttering a little, she slipped the key from his pocket, trying to focus on the present situation and not his hunkiness quotient. She turned and gathered the morphine and IV materials and came back to the whimpering boy, wanting to ease his pain quickly.

"Tell him he'll feel a little pinch then I'm going to put a straw in his hand that'll make his leg hurt less," she said, concentrating on getting the IV going fast.

"Damn," Chase said.

She looked up and saw him shaking his head. "What?"

"I'd forgotten how good you are at that. One stick and, *bam*, the IV's in. I don't think he even felt it."

His voice and expression were filled with admiration, which made her feel absurdly pleased. "Thanks."

He leaned closer. "He's lucky you're here."

"And he's lucky to have you to put his leg back together."

He smiled and she smiled back, her breath catching at how ridiculously handsome the man looked when his eyes were all fudgy brown and warm and his lips teasingly curved.

"The little girl's going to get the world's most meticulous stitcher-upper, too," Chase said, still smiling as he tweezed out lingering pieces of gravel from Apollo's wound. "I remember a button you sewed so tightly on my shirt I couldn't get it through the little hole any more."

"Well, I only did it for you because, considering you're a surgeon, you're really bad at sewing on buttons."

His eyes crinkled at the corners as they met hers again, and her heart skipped a beat, darn it all. With the IV in place, the boy's eyes drooped as the morphine took effect. Chase placed an X-ray plate under the boy's calf, then rolled a machine across the room, positioning its C-arm over his shin, obviously suspecting, as she did, that it also might be broken.

"Is the X-ray tech coming soon?"

"No X-ray tech. Honduras was loaded with staff compared to this place. I'll get this film developing before I work on the compound fracture."

Wow. Hard to believe they had to take and develop the X-rays. "I'll get started with the girl. Where's irrigation?"

He nodded toward the wide, low sink. "Faucet. The secret to pollution is dilution. It's the best we have."

Her eyes widened. "Seriously? I stick her wounds under the faucet?"

"Attach the hose. We've found it provides more force than the turkey basters we use on less polluted wounds. It's how I'm going to get him cleaned up now that he's had pain meds. You're not in Kansas any more, Toto. Be right back." With a wink, he left with the X-ray cartridge in his hand.

Dani grabbed a pair of sterile gloves from a box attached to the wall and rolled a stool from under the counter to sit next to the gurney. She smiled at the wide-eyed girl and her mother.

If only she spoke their language, or even a little French. The girl looked scared but wasn't shedding a single tear. Hopefully, when the local nurse arrived, she could interpret for Dani. Or Chase would. One of the many amazing things about the darned man was all the languages he could speak fluently or partially. He had a true gift for it, while Dani hated the fact that it had never come easily to her.

"I'm going to wash—*laver*—her cuts to get all the gravel and nasty stuff out of there." Lord, was that the only French word she could come up with?

The mother seemed to understand, though, nodding gravely. Dani rolled the gurney to the low sink and couldn't believe she had to stick the child's various extremities practically inside it, scrubbing with good old antiseptic soap to clean out the debris. Thank goodness the numbing solution seemed to be working pretty well, as the scrubbing didn't seem to hurt her patient too badly.

"You're being very brave," she told the little

girl, who gave her a shy smile in return, though she probably didn't understand the words.

The mother helped with the washing, and Dani thought about how her own perspective had changed since she'd had Drew. When she had been in med school, and then when she'd become a doctor, she'd thought she'd got it. But now she truly understood how terrifying it must be to have your child seriously injured or ill.

When Chase returned, Dani had finished prepping the girl and helped him get the boy's wounds washed out. Not an easy task, because tiny bits of gravel seemed determined to stay embedded in his flesh. Thank heavens the morphine made the situation tolerable for the child.

"You want me to stitch this big lac on his head, or do you want to do it after I work on his leg?" Chase asked, then grinned. "Or maybe we should call in the plastic surgeon."

"Funny. I'm as good as any plastic surgeon anyway. Tell his mom he'll be as handsome as ever when I'm done."

Chase chatted with the mother as they laid the boy back on the gurney, and the woman managed a smile, her lips trembling and tears filling her eyes for a moment.

"I haven't seen anything like this since Honduras," Dani said quietly to Chase as they got the patient comfortable and increased his morphine drip in preparation for setting the leg. "Been in a suburban practice where the bad stuff goes to the ER. The roughest stuff I dealt with was ear infections."

"So you're sorry you came?"

"No." She shook her head and gave him a crooked smile. "Even though you're here, I'd almost forgotten how much we're needed in places like this."

"Except you shouldn't have brought Drew. Which we'll be talking about." His expression hardened.

Oh, right. Those deep, dark issues they had to deal with separate from what they were doing now.

Yes, Chase was a great surgeon and good man, but she had to remember why she'd left in the first place. Because he didn't want a child. And she wasn't about to let him bully her into doing things his way and only his way, without regard for how it would affect Drew.

Glad to be able to put some physical distance between them to go with the emotional distance that had suddenly appeared, she stepped away to stitch the girl's cuts.

"I'm taking him into the OR to set the bone and put a transverse pin in the distal femur," Chase said, wheeling the gurney to the swinging door that led to the operating room. "If Trent comes down, tell him I'm just going to splint it and put drains in for now, until the swelling goes down. When the nurse anesthetist gets here, tell her to grab the X-rays and come in."

He stopped to place his hand on the mother's shoulder, speaking to her in the soothing, warm tones that always reassured patients and family and had been known to weaken Dani's knees. From now on, though, when it came to Chase, she had to be sure her knees, and every other part of her, stayed strong.

"Once you heal, it's going to take a while to get your leg strong again. But I promise we'll help you with exercises for that, and you'll be playing soccer again in no time." Chase smiled at the boy, now in a hospital bed with a trapeze apparatus connected to his leg with a counterweight, which had to feel really miserable in the hot, un-air-conditioned hospital ward.

Lucky, really, that it wasn't a whole lot worse, with bad internal injuries. Barring some hard-to-control infection, he'd eventually be running again. Damned drunk driver apparently hadn't even seen the poor kids. Chase's lips tightened.

As Chase suspected, in addition to the compound fracture, the boy's tibia had been broken too, and he'd put a cast on it before finally getting him set up in bed. It would be damned uncomfortable for the kid, but would keep the bones immobile so he could begin to heal.

"Nice work, Dr. Sheridan," he said to Dani as he looked closely at the boy's forehead, which she'd nearly finished stitching. Dani looked up at him from her sitting position next to the bed, a light glow of perspiration on her beautiful face. Her blue, blue eyes smiled at him in a way that made him want to pick up where they'd left off the night before. If they'd been alone, he would have. Convincing her to marry him was a pleasure he looked forward to. Except he needed to stop thinking about all the ways he planned to accomplish that before everyone in the room knew where his thoughts had travelled.

He could tell Dani already did. "I've always appreciated the superior techniques you implement for everything you do," he said, giving her a wicked grin.

Her smile faded and her fair skin turned deeply pink, and she quickly turned to finish working on the boy's forehead. He nearly laughed, pleased at how easily he could still rattle her.

The nasty gash was now a thin red line within the tiny stitches Dani was currently tying off. If anything, she'd gotten even better at it than when they'd been in Honduras. Even back then he'd been amazed at her talent for leaving only the smallest scar.

"Tell him he looks very handsome and rugged, like a pirate," she said, smiling at the boy. "His friends will be jealous."

Chase translated and the kid managed a small smile, but his mother laughed, the sound full of relief. She'd been fanning the child practically non-stop with a home-made fan, trying to keep him comfortable in the stifling heat of the room and to ward off pesky flies that always found their way into the hospital ward, regardless of everyone's efforts to keep them out.

They'd set Apollo's sister up in the bed next to him, though she didn't really need to stay in for observation. Their mother, though, would be bringing food in for her son and sleeping next to him on the floor to help care for him, so it made sense to keep the little girl here too, as the bed was available.

"We'll be putting a new cast on his whole leg some time after the swelling goes down, but for now we'll be keeping him comfortable with some pain medicine," he said to the mother. "I'll be back later to check on him."

He tipped his neck from side to side to release the kinks that always tightened there after a long procedure. With everything they could do for the kids finished for now, he felt suddenly anxious to find Drew and tell him the truth. He gathered up Dani's suture kit. "Ready to go, Doctor?"

"Not really," she mumbled under her breath as she stripped off her gloves.

She looked up at him as she stood, her face full of the same uncertainty and anxiety that had been there earlier. Why was she so worried about telling their son that he was the boy's father? If she didn't look so sweet and vulnerable, he'd be insulted.

Sure, he'd said he didn't want kids, but that had been before he'd known it was already moot.

She'd see how good it would be. He'd reassure her, romance her, be a good dad to Drew, and she'd realize that everything would be okay. His mood lifted, became downright buoyant, and he tugged at one of the crazy blonde curls that had escaped from her ponytail.

Last night when he'd kissed her, she hadn't been able to hide that she still wanted him the way he wanted her. She'd come round. Marry him. He'd find a good job for her in the States where he could work sometimes, too, and Drew would be safe.

Yeah, it was a good plan. He knew he could make it happen.

He tugged another curl.

"You know, you're like a second-grader some-times," she said, pulling her head away with a frown. "Next, you'll be putting a frog down my shirt."

"No. A lizard." He folded her soft hand into his. "Let's find Drew."

CHAPTER FOUR

"THIS LOOKS LIKE a good lizard spot." Chase maneuvered the Land Rover off the dusty road and around some scrub towards a grouping of rocks.

"I can't believe you're really planning on catching one," Dani said, shaking her head. "I know you have quick reflexes, but I think even you are a little slower than a lizard. And if you do catch one, it'll probably bite you."

"Watch and learn." He grinned at Dani but the smile she gave in return was very half-hearted, and shadows touched the blue of her eyes. He stuffed down his impatience to tell Drew and get it over with so she'd relax and see what a great dad he was going to be. So she'd get over her illogical attitude and say yes to marrying him.

Chase stopped the vehicle by the rocks, which would hopefully prove to be a good hiding place for the reptiles. Not that the primary reason for coming out this afternoon was really about lizards. But he wanted Drew to like him and remembered how much fun he'd had searching for lizards and various other creatures with his own dad and brother.

"Spud packed an old blanket we can use as a sort of tablecloth on the rock," Chase said. He turned to the child sitting in the car seat in the back. Every time he looked at the boy the wonder and worry over having a child slammed him in the chest all over again. "How about a snack, Drew? Then we'll go hunting."

"I'll get the picnic bag Spud put together for us," Dani said.

He watched Dani slide from the front seat, enjoying the view of her perfect, sexy behind in her khaki shorts. Her lean, toned legs. She opened the back door and unlatched their son from his car seat.

His son. Such a crazy word to think. To have rolling from his lips when he'd been alone and tried out how it would feel to say it. *My son.* But none of it was as strange as how normal it felt to look at the child and know Drew was his. To feel the strong tug of emotion that pulled at his heart for the sweet-faced boy he barely knew.

If Drew wouldn't have balked at it, Chase would've taken his son from the seat himself and carried him to stand tall on the biggest rock where they planned to enjoy a picnic before going lizard hunting. Now that he knew about Drew, it felt oddly natural to be a father, and that itself seemed more than surprising.

During his run this morning, he'd found himself thinking of all the things he wanted to do with Drew. All the things he'd loved as a kid. All the things his own father had shared with him, taught him. Except so many of those things stemmed from having lived in other places and cultures around the world. He'd have to figure out which of those things they'd be able to do together in the States, where Drew belonged.

While he'd never been particularly comfortable in the U.S., he was more than willing to work there part of the year to spend time with his child and his wife. Seeing them every day while he was there would make it worthwhile. And with global communications being what they were these days, it would be easy to stay in touch, even close, when he worked missions.

He knew in his bones it would work out fine for everyone. His family.

Chase grabbed the blanket from the back of the car, along with a wooden box he'd brought for any lizards they'd manage to catch.

The savannah stretched for as far as they could see to the hilly horizon, with scruffy trees here and there amid lush grasses and brown scrub. He headed to a nice, flat rock perfect for a picnic and began to lay the blanket across it.

"Let me help." A few soft, blonde curls that had escaped Dani's ponytail fell across her cheek as she leaned over the rock. He wanted to drop the corner he was holding and feel them wrapped around his finger. Tickle the shell of her ear as he tucked them there. Bring her mouth to his.

She doesn't like it when you push. He grabbed one end of the fabric and together they smoothed it across the rock. Or attempted to smooth it, with Drew scrabbling across the rock on all fours looking a bit like a crab and bunching up the blanket until Dani grabbed him up and swung him in circles.

"We can't eat with you messing up the blanket, silly."

"I a lizard!" Drew protested as Dani set him on his feet and kissed the top of his head.

"I know. And I have yummy bugs to feed you if you sit on the rock like a good reptile."

"Okay. I like bugs." Drew quickly climbed onto the rock and sat, comically sticking out his tongue and giggling.

Chase and Dani both chuckled. The kid was so damned cute. He and Dani reached for the food bag at the same time, and her eyes met and locked with his. For a moment they just stared at one another, and Chase nearly reached for her, wanting to kiss away the worry behind her smile and whatever other emotions he saw flickering in their blue depths. The beautiful blue he'd seen so many times in his dreams after she'd left Honduras.

He gave up resisting and lifted his hand to cup her cheek, placing a quick, gentle kiss on her soft lips. "Why so gloomy? The Dani I remember was full of sass and saw everything as an adventure. Not a worrywart," he said. "You've been adventuring with Drew alone. All I want is to jump in and join you."

She gave him a twisted smile and shook her head. "Maybe today. But what about tomorrow? What about next year, when you're who-knows-where and have forgotten all about us?"

What a damned insulting thing to say. As though he'd ever forget all about them. "If you'll just—"

"I want my bugs!" Drew began lizard-walking again, sticking out his tongue and tangling the blanket.

"Okay, lizard-boy. Let's see what's in here." Chase huffed out a frustrated breath at both her attitude and his apparent inability to just shut up about the subject for one minute.

Except he knew why he'd opened his mouth. He'd wanted to wipe that worry from her face. Wanted to see the sunny, vibrant Dani again. But pushing her was the wrong approach, and he knew it. Showing her his commitment to making a marriage and family work was the way to convince her, not with words. Not by getting irritated with her doubts, which he supposed he couldn't blame her for having.

He pulled out the grilled chicken on sticks that Spud always made and looked to see what else was in the bag. "Here are the best-tasting bugs in Benin," Chase said, pulling a box of raisins from the sack. Drew sat back on his haunches and opened his mouth. They began a comical game, with Chase tossing the raisins into Drew's mouth and the child slurping up any that fell onto the blanket.

"Okay, you two. Even lizards need more substantial food than bugs," Dani said.

She put the rest of the picnic on metal plates. "What's this stuff?" she asked, lifting the foil from a plastic bowl to expose soft, lumpy, brown and beige discs.

"Those are *akara*," Chase said. "Fried fritters made from black-eyed peas. They're kind of ugly but they're good."

Dani handed one to Drew as she assembled a few other things on the child's plate. Holding it in both hands, he took a big bite then promptly spit it out right onto the blanket, leaving his tongue hanging from his mouth with a comical look of anguish on his face. "Cookie yucky!"

Chase didn't want Drew to think they were laughing at his distress, and tried to keep his face from showing how hilarious the poor kid's expression was. "Sorry, buddy. That's not a cookie. Guess we should have made that clearer."

"Poor Drew. Have a drink to wash it down." Dani handed him a water bottle and wiped up the food. Apparently she wasn't too worried about Drew being offended, as a laugh bubbled from her lips, and the sound of her amusement stole Chase's breath. He looked at the curve of her sexy lips and the sparkle in her beautiful eyes, beyond relieved that she was finally more relaxed and happy.

He'd always loved her laugh, her smile, her sense of humor. Kissing that laughing mouth was almost as high on his agenda as telling Drew that he was his father, but he reminded himself he had to go slowly.

But not too slowly. Who knew when his next assignment would come through? The thought of having to leave before Dani believed in their relationship again scared the hell out of him.

After they'd eaten, Chase grasped Dani's hand to let her know the time had come to tell Drew, together. Instantly, a grim expression replaced the soft happiness on her face of just a moment ago, and he shoved down the disappointment he felt at the transformation. What had he ever done to make her look at him like that?

"Andrew." The child stopped banging a stick against the rock and looked up at him expectantly. Chase figured he should take the lead in this, as he had a feeling Dani would be as tongue-tied as she'd been earlier if he left it all up to her. "This morning your mom was telling you she brought you to Africa for two reasons. Besides helping kids here, she wanted you to meet me. And I really wanted to meet you."

He looked at her and the worry—damn it, he'd even call it torment—in her eyes made him pause. Did she need to be the one to say it?

"Yes, Drew." Her voice sounded strained and her grip on his hand tightened. "I'm so happy because, believe it or not, you finally get to meet your daddy. Dr. Chase is your daddy. Isn't that great?"

To Chase's shock, her lips quivered and fat tears filled her eyes and spilled over. She quickly swiped them away, but not before they hit him hard in the gut.

Dani wasn't an over-emotional woman, crying over any little thing. That she was moved to tears now showed him what he hadn't even thought about. How hard all this had been on her, no doubt from the beginning. Being pregnant with Drew, alone. Giving birth to him, alone. Raising him, alone.

Painful guilt swamped him. No, he hadn't known about Drew. But he should have been more intuitive when she'd proposed to him, damn it. And it had been his words that had driven her to secrecy.

He wrapped his arm around her shoulders and pulled her close, kissing her salty cheek and giving her a smile he hoped would show her that her solitary hardship was over. That, even when she was in the States while he worked elsewhere, she would never be truly alone.

He looked at Drew, whose head was tipped to one side, his big brown eyes studying Chase. "Your mom told me you're the best boy in the whole world, and I'm incredibly lucky to be your dad. I'm really happy to get to spend time with you now."

Drew looked at his mother then jumped off the rock to start banging the stick on it again. "I thought maybe Mr. Matt was gonna be my daddy."

Mr. Matt? Chase stiffened and his arm dropped from Dani's shoulder. Was Dani involved with someone? His brain froze. Why hadn't he even thought to wonder? Or ask?

A short, uncomfortable laugh left Dani's lips. "Mr. Matt is just a friend. Dr. Chase is your daddy, and I think he'd like it if you called him that."

"Yes, I'd like that, Drew." He only half heard himself speak. What the hell was he going to do if Dani was in love with someone else? A strange sensation gripped his heart that was panic and anger combined. They had a son together, and she belonged to him. It would be over Chase's dead body if another man tried to claim her. Tried to make decisions that affected Drew. That affected where his son lived and who he lived with.

"'K.'" Drew smiled then shrieked. "A lizard! Look!"

The boy ran, chasing a tiny lizard through and around the rocks, and Chase turned to Dani, trying to speak past the tightness gripping his throat and squeezing his chest.

"What the hell? Do you have a boyfriend?"

"What do you mean, 'What the hell?'" Dani said, frowning. "You act like you and I were still together. In case you've forgotten, we'd both moved on with our lives until yesterday."

The primitive possessiveness that roared through his blood shocked him in its intensity. "You can tell this Mr. Matt to get lost. That you're getting married."

She looked at him like she thought he was crazy. Which was fine, because he suddenly felt a little crazy. She made him crazy.

"I'm pretty sure I already told you I'm not marrying you. Can't you just stop with the full court press and get to know Drew? Like I said, we'll work out a solution where you can spend time with him each year."

"Are you—?" Chase realized he was practically shouting and lowered his voice. "Are you in love with this guy?"

"My feelings for Matt are irrelevant. What is relevant is figuring out how to make sure Drew knows he's important to you. That he's not just some in-the-way, annoying afterthought in your life."

He grasped her shoulders in his hands and pulled her close. "You know, I'm getting damned tired of you implying I'm going to be a deadbeat, rotten, selfish father. I've known Drew barely one day, but if you don't think I'd throw myself in front of a truck for him, you don't know me at all."

She drew a deep breath, and stared at him searchingly as she slowly released it. "Okay. I'm sorry. Let's…let's just enjoy the day with Drew. We'll figure out the rest later."

Jealousy and frustration wouldn't let him agree. He glanced over at Drew to see him occupied, enthusiastically poking his stick into a crack in a rock. "Is this Matt guy the reason you won't agree to marry me?"

"No. I won't marry you for all the reasons I've already said. I believe two people should get married because they want to live together and be together and love one another. Not so you can call the shots or because it's a logical course of action."

There was damned well nothing logical about the way he was feeling. Nothing very mature or sophisticated either. He wanted to throw her over his shoulder and make her his right then and there. Then he wanted to find this Matt guy and punch him in the face. But since he couldn't do either of those things, he settled for the one thing he could do.

He pulled her tightly against him and kissed her. Without finesse. Without thoughts of reminding her what they'd had three years ago. He kissed her with the anger and fear and uncertainty that pummeled his heart. He kissed her with the release of a deep and pent-up hunger for her he hadn't even realized was there until she'd come back into his life.

Her palms pushed against his chest and she pulled her mouth from his. She stared at him, both confusion and desire swimming in her eyes. The memories of past kisses, of yesterday and of three years ago, crackled between them. Her breath mingled with his. Her clean, sweet scent enveloped him. And there was no way he could keep from taking her mouth with his again.

This time her palms swept up his chest, her cool fingers slid across his nape. A low moan sounded deep in her throat, and he tasted the same wild desire on her tongue that surged through every nerve in his body. He cupped the back of her head, tangling his fingers in her thick hair, wanting to release her ponytail and feel those crazy curls slide across his skin.

The anger, the jealousy that had shoved him headlong into the kiss faded. Replaced by the warm and heady craving that had always burned between them. The taste of her, filled with a soul-deep passion and the promise of intimate pleasures only she could give.

He let his hand wander, cupping her bottom and pressing her against him. Her heat sent his thigh nudging between her legs and he felt her respond by rubbing against him, a sweet murmur of pleasure vibrating from her lips to his.

"Mommy! I catched the lizard! I catched it!"

They pulled apart, and he was sure he wore the same shocked and slightly horrified expression she did. Both their chests were heaving with rapid breaths, and she lifted shaking fingers to her lips as she turned towards Drew.

Damn. Chase scrubbed his hand across his face. He'd like to think he would have remembered Drew was there. That he wouldn't have put his hand up her shirt or down her pants or any of the many things he'd been about to do. But he had to grimly admit that he'd been so far gone, he just might have done any and all of it anyway.

He'd have to be more careful. Remember there were three of them now, not just him and Dani. Of course, she'd goaded him into it with the whole thing about her refusal to marry him. Her damned boyfriend.

But with that thought came a smile of grim satisfaction. If Dani thought she was in love with this Matt guy, the spontaneous combustion they'd just shared had surely proved her wrong. The way it had always been between them, from the very first weeks they'd met.

"Chase!"

Dani's slightly panicky voice had him quickly heading to her and Drew.

"Chase, are you sure these things don't bite? I think you should drop it, Drew. Now."

"No. It mine." The boy's chin jutted mulishly. "Daddy said we could catch some."

Daddy. To hear Drew call him that in such a natural way, like they hadn't met just yesterday, was inconceivable yet wonderful, and the tight band constricting his chest eased slightly.

The boy's stubby little fingers grasped the tail of a lizard no bigger than a mouse as it writhed to get loose. He had to chuckle at the triumph on Drew's face and the distaste on Dani's.

"A master lizard-catcher. Like father, like son." Yeah, the boy was a true Bowen. If only his brother was here to share the moment.

The thought brought his enjoyment down a notch, at the same time reinforcing exactly why he was adamant that Drew grow up in the U.S.

He reached for the wooden box he'd found at the compound. "Here, Drew, I brought this to put it in. We can only keep it for a day then we'll let it go so it stays healthy. Okay?"

"Okay." Drew dropped it into the box, a huge grin on his face. "I a good lizard-hunter, aren't I?"

"The best." Chase's heart filled with something powerful and unfamiliar as he looked at the boy's adorable little face, lit with the kind of joy unique to children. Drew's smile was blinding. The boy might look like him, but that beautiful smile was all Dani.

He lifted his gaze to Dani's and their eyes locked in a wordless connection. So many emotions flickered in her eyes. Wariness, apprehension, anxiety. Warring with the remnants of their intoxicating kiss. His gaze dropped to her full lips, still moist, and it was all he could do not to grab her and start what they hadn't been able to finish.

He forced himself to step back and give her the breathing room, the time she'd asked for. Waiting wasn't one of the things he was best at, but he'd try. With maybe just a little nudge to shorten the wait.

* * *

"So, is there any chance you and Dad can make it down here?" Finally, his mother had returned his call. Chase had begun to wonder if something was wrong, or if they'd left Senegal and hadn't told him, with sketchy cell service somewhere remote.

"We'd love to see you, honey. It so happens we have a few days off," his mother's voice said in his ear. "But it's usually me trying to get us together, not you. Anything going on?"

"Actually, yes." He paced in his room, still undecided whether he should tell them about Drew over the phone or just let them meet him.

"Well? Are you going to tell me or keep me in suspense?"

He wasn't sure exactly what to say but decided he should just let them know so they'd be prepared. "I want you to meet your grandson. Andrew. He's two and a half and cute as can be."

There was a long silence, and Chase could just picture his mother's stunned expression. Probably similar to his when he'd first seen the boy who looked exactly like him and his brother.

"Are you there?" he asked.

"Yes. It's just that I thought you said I have a grandson. A grandson?"

Her voice rose in pitch, and Chase was pretty sure it was with excitement. Of course she'd be excited. Both his parents loved children and knew he'd always said he'd never have kids. Most likely, this was a dream-come-true for her.

"Yes. I just found out… It's kind of a long story. But Drew's mother is here with me, and we're getting married soon." True, she hadn't yet agreed to that. But if he had to move mountains, she would. And having his parents come was another step towards convincing her. They'd love Dani and Drew, and she'd love them, too. It would give her a chance to see how good they'd be as a family.

"Oh, Chase, I can't believe it!" His mother laughed, and obviously pulled her mouth from the phone as she spoke to his dad. "Phil! Phil, we have a grandson! Get on the internet and book a flight to Benin right now."

Chase grinned. He'd had a feeling his mom would drop everything to meet Drew.

"Let me know when you're going to get here, and I'll try to pick you up from the airport. Or Spud will, if I can't get away."

"Okay. Oh, goodness, I can't wait to get there. I'm off to pack. Bye."

She hung up without even waiting for a response, and the disturbing feelings he'd had ever since he'd heard about this Matt character eased a little. Not only would his mom and dad embrace his son and hopefully soon-to-be wife, he'd recruit them to emphasize to Dani how important it was to keep Drew in the U.S. until he was older. Maybe she'd listen to two experienced mission doctors who happened to be Drew's grandparents in a way she wasn't currently listening to him.

The little nudge named Evelyn Bowen was on her way.

CHAPTER FIVE

WITH CHASE MYSTERIOUSLY gone somewhere, Dani sat in the empty clinic room and tried to focus on the sketchy and incomplete care and immunization records. She was working to get them organized and into the laptop computer she'd brought from the States—fairly unsuccessfully, since she kept wondering where Chase had gone. Kept thinking about the charm he'd been intent on oozing nonstop since yesterday when they'd told Drew that Chase was his daddy.

Kept reliving the feel of his stolen kisses against her cheek or the side of her neck whenever they were together, his fingertips sliding across the skin of her arms. How had she not known her arms were an erogenous zone?

They probably weren't, unless it was Chase touching her. She couldn't help but respond to his teasing caress, the curve of his lips, the sensual promise in the chocolaty depths of his eyes.

She huffed out a frustrated breath. Why, oh, why did she have such a hard time steeling herself against the man's sexual energy and tempting persuasion?

She'd been relieved at how easily Drew had accepted that Chase was his daddy. But, of course, she'd known he was so young he wouldn't have many questions about it. She'd hoped they could tell Drew then ease into a new relationship as two parents living separate lives, with the best interests of their child the only personal connection between them.

But what happened instead? She'd fallen into his embrace, into his kiss, with barely one second of resistance. Her cheeks burned with embarrassment. Especially because his kiss certainly hadn't been full of tenderness. It had been full of anger and possessiveness, no doubt because Drew had mentioned Matt and a competitive man like Chase wouldn't just shrug at something like that.

No, she had a feeling that had just added more

fuel to the hot fire already burning within Chase about the two of them getting married.

Matt was the first man she'd dated since Chase, since leaving Honduras to go back to the States to work and start a new life there with Drew. Having a man in her life hadn't been on her to-do list. But Matt had seemed so easygoing, so harmless, really, that she'd finally given in to going out with him a few times the month before she'd left for Benin. He'd been happy to include Drew in several excursions and had been pleasant to spend time with.

Kissing him had been pleasant, too. Pleasant, but not knee-weakening. Not breathtaking. Not so mesmerizing that she'd forget everything except how his mouth tasted and her heart pounded and how much she wanted to get naked and intimate the way she had when Chase had kissed her. So all-consuming that she'd lost all thought about anything but the way he'd made her feel.

And that was bad. In so many ways. More than bad that she hadn't spared one thought about Drew seeing them devouring one another and rubbing their bodies together. Her face burned all over again at the thought, even though Drew was too young to think much of it, even if he'd noticed.

It was bad because she had to keep her focus. She had to resist the intense, overpowering attraction she'd felt for Chase since practically the first moment she'd met him and which clearly hadn't gone away with time and distance.

As she'd told him before, great sex wasn't a reason to get married. Neither was a feeling of obligation on Chase's part. Or a need to control their lives. If she ever did marry, she wanted it to be because her husband loved her more than anything. Wanted to be with her more than anything. Believed she was every bit as important to him as his work.

And that obviously just wasn't true with Chase.

Love had nothing to do with him wanting marriage, and she shoved away the deep stab of pain that knowledge caused. His reasoning that she and Drew should stay in the States while he lived his life the way he always had, or close to it, just wasn't enough. Not for her and not for Drew.

Working with underprivileged people around

the world was important to her, especially after she'd seen all the need in Honduras. She had her career plan all worked out, where she'd be employed in the U.S. for two years, spend nine months abroad, then head back to the States for two more years. And giving Drew exposure to other cultures couldn't be anything but good for him.

Not to mention that, if Chase was still going to live all over the world, it made no sense to get married and pretend they were a family the years they lived in the U.S. Didn't he see that Drew would always know he wasn't as important to his dad as his job? But if they weren't married, Drew would accept that his parents were no longer together, and would understand why his dad lived somewhere else.

She believed Chase when he said he wanted to be part of Drew's life. It would probably work out okay if he saw Drew several times a year for a few weeks each time. After all, they lived in a global world now. With phone calls and video chats online, being close to one another shouldn't be too hard.

What a tangled mess. But she was here to do a job, not think endlessly about the problems. She stared at the scribbled index cards, and wondered why some of the previous doctors and nurses had even bothered to record the unreadable notes.

"Dani, are you in here?"

"Yes." She absolutely wouldn't ask Chase where he'd gone. For all she knew, he'd been seeing a woman. And it was none of her business.

Chase strode into the room, looking so good in jeans and a pale yellow polo shirt that showed off his tanned skin and dark hair and eyes that she caught herself staring. She pulled her gaze back to the cards, typing what she could into the computer.

"Making progress?" he asked, leaning over her to look at her work, resting his palm between her shoulder blades.

"Not much. I can't even read most of them. We're just going to have to start with new records of children as we see them." She stared fixedly at her work. "I'd like to talk with you about ways we can get parents to bring their kids in for checks."

"It's not easy. A lot of folks don't have transportation, so they only come when there's a serious problem. Some believe Vodun will keep their children from getting sick."

"Vodun?"

"Voodoo. The word translates as 'spirit.'" His hand slid up her back to cup the back of her neck, his breath whispering across her cheek. "We'll talk about all that when we go into the field soon to do immunizations in various villages."

His mouth dropped to caress the skin beneath her earlobe, which sent a delicious shiver across her throat until she jerked her head away.

"You know, back home that would be considered sexual harassment. Don't make me contact the GPC to lodge a complaint."

"You think a tiny kiss is sexual harassment?" His low laugh vibrated against her skin. "I can think of lots more ways to harass you sexually. If you ask nicely."

"You're ridiculous." She shook her head, feeling slightly dizzy. She should be annoyed, but instead had to desperately will herself to be tough and strong against the seductive temptation of his lips. "In case you haven't noticed, I'm trying to work here. Leave me alone. Seriously."

To her surprise and relief, he straightened and his warm hand left her nape. "Take a break from that for a minute. Ruth and Drew need you to come outside."

"Why?" She swiveled to look at him. He had an odd expression on his face, slightly amused and clearly anticipatory. Obviously nothing was wrong and her curiosity was piqued, in spite of herself.

"You'll see. Come on."

He grasped her hand and she rose from the chair, tugging her hand from his as she followed him out the clinic doors.

As they approached the small enclosure that served as a playground for patients' children and siblings, she could see Drew scooting around on a plastic ride-on toy train that hadn't been there earlier, a wide grin on his face. And two people standing next to him with equally ecstatic expressions.

Who...?

"Toot-toot! Toot-toot!" Drew exclaimed, scuffing his shoes in the dirt as he rode.

Chase put his arm across Dani's shoulders before they stepped inside the gate of the wooden fence. "Mom and Dad, I'd like you to meet Dr. Danielle Sheridan. Dani, my parents, Drs. Philip and Evelyn Bowen."

His parents. Drew's grandparents. Stunned, Dani smiled and reached to shake Chase's father's hand. "It's nice to meet you." Nice and shocking. They just popped in for a quick trip to Benin to meet Drew?

About to shake Evelyn's hand, the woman gave her a warm embrace instead. "It's so delightful to meet you, dear. And our Andrew is so adorable. Precious! I can't believe how he looks just like Chase did at that age. You have no idea how happy you've made us."

Our Andrew. The words put a funny little flutter of joy in Dani's chest. She had to smile at the lovely woman's greeting and obvious sincerity. How wonderful that Andrew had grandparents who would clearly want to be a part of his life. Her own mother lived pretty far from where Dani had gotten a job and, as a nurse, worked a lot of hours. Not the kind of grandmother who would be baking cookies and babysitting.

Then again, neither were the Drs. Bowen, working in mission hospitals around the world. Nonetheless, it was nice.

"I'm…surprised you're here," Dani said, giving Chase a look he couldn't misinterpret. He responded with a grin that showed no guilty feelings at all about his subterfuge. "Where do you live?"

"We're working in Senegal right now. Benin's a pretty quick airplane ride from there, really." The woman clasped her hands together, her eyes sparkling. "When Chase told us about Drew and you, we were over the moon. We brought the little train and a few other gifts. I hope that's okay?"

"Of course." Dani smiled. "But I can't tell if he likes it or not, can you?"

They all chuckled, as it was more than obvious he loved it. Scooting around, toot-tooting endlessly and grinning.

"They'd barely taken it from the box before he jumped on it," Chase said as he watched Drew, his gaze soft with a hint of pride. "He's going to be riding a bike in no time."

"We're happy he likes it," Phil said. "I'm especially pleased because if he didn't, I have a feeling Evelyn and I would be heading straight to another store to look for something else, even if we had to fly to Cotonou. I kept having to remind her we were bringing everything on a plane, she had so much stuff."

"It's a grandparents' prerogative to buy their grandchildren presents," Evelyn said, an indulgent smile on her face as she watched Drew. "Especially the very first one."

First one? She couldn't know Chase's attitude about having children if she thought there would ever be more.

That thought led Dani in a nasty and very uncomfortable direction it hadn't gone before, making her stiffen. What if Chase did marry someday? What kind of woman would be stepmother to Drew? Just thinking about it made her stomach twist. She reminded herself he'd be working in remote places around the world, so Drew wouldn't be around a stepmother much anyway, but didn't succeed in ridding herself of a slightly sick feeling in her gut.

Evelyn turned her attention to Dani. "I hear there's to be a wedding soon. Have you decided on a date?"

What? One look at Chase proved he really had told his parents they were getting married. How arrogant could the man be? He had an infuriatingly smug smile on his face, and an expression that said he couldn't wait to see how she'd react to his mother's question.

"A wedding? I hadn't heard about one. Is it someone I know?" She kept her voice light, her expression bland, but knew Chase could see the challenge in her gaze. So he thought this was one big chess game? He'd forgotten she'd learned to play from him.

His parents looked at one another then at Chase, obviously confused. "Chase said—"

"I said we were getting married. I didn't say Dani had agreed yet," Chase said smoothly, with a look that said, *Answer that.* "But wouldn't it be great to make it happen some time when you could be here to share it with us? Please help me convince her how nice it would be to celebrate our marriage as a family."

Damn the man. He'd certainly played his turn well, with both his parents staring at her with bemused expressions.

"Chase and I just recently met up again," she said, trying to figure out exactly what to say. It was a battle to keep from narrowing her eyes and scowling at Chase for putting her in such an awkward position. Though she was pretty sure that, even if they didn't know the details of her relationship with Chase, his parents knew how babies were made. "I don't feel we know each other well enough again to consider something as important as marriage."

Both his parents looked back at Chase, and Dani felt a slightly hysterical desire to laugh, thinking they looked like they were watching a tennis match.

"All I want is for the three of us to be a family, and I'm sure you'd agree that's the best thing for Drew. But Dani's being difficult." Chase rocked back on his heels, his hands in his jeans pockets. "It's hard to believe, because any woman would be lucky to put my ring on her finger, right, Mom?"

That smile continued to play about his lips. He'd always been good at that delicate combination of joking humor while making a very serious point.

Dani looked at Evelyn, figuring that, as his mother, she doubtless agreed he was an awesome catch for any woman.

"Dr. Bowen, I…" Dani began, not even sure what she was going to say.

"Please, call me Evelyn." She reached to squeeze Dani's arm. "Pay no attention to Chase's heavy-handed attempts at manipulation. I'm surprised, really, at his clumsiness. From the time he was little, he could get whatever he wanted without anyone even knowing he was leading them there."

Astonished at his mother's words, Dani was also more than amused at the surprised and outraged expression on Chase's face.

"What the hell?" He folded his arms across his chest. "You don't think Dani should marry me? What about Drew? What about us being a family?"

"Don't drag your father and me into this." His mother held up her hand. "Obviously, there's some reason you didn't even know about Drew until now. While we'd love to welcome Dani as our daughter-in-law, you two will have to figure all this out on your own. As long as I get to play doting grandmother to our darling baby, I'm happy."

Phil chuckled. "And I have a feeling that 'doting' will be an understatement."

Evelyn grasped Phil's hand and they walked over to stand on either side of Drew, forming a bridge with their arms. "Drive through the tunnel, engineer Andrew. But watch out, there might be a landslide and it could collapse on you," Phil said.

Drew shrieked in delight as he drove around their legs and through the "tunnel," ending up trapped as their arms surrounded him.

As she watched them, Dani's heart filled with how lovely Chase's parents were and how lucky Drew was that they wanted to be a part of his life, even though their time together would doubtless be infrequent.

"I can't believe this," Chase said.

She looked at his disgusted scowl and knew he wasn't talking about his parents' game with Drew. "Is this finally the proof you need that you should get over the unpleasant controlling streak you have? Even your mother thinks so."

"She didn't say I'm controlling. And I'm not."

He stepped close and she was glad his parents were here. Surely Chase wouldn't touch her and kiss her and make her feel all weak and out of control while they were around.

"But convincing?" His mouth came close to her ear, and he smelled so good, like fresh soap and aftershave and him, that it was all she could do not to turn her head for a kiss anyway. "Convincing you will be a pleasure."

He backed off a few inches, and the promise in his dark eyes told her resistance would be tough going. But she could do it. She *would* do it. To protect Drew and to protect her own heart.

"Lunch, everybody!" Spud bellowed from the door.

Drew jumped off the plastic train, knocking it over onto its side, and ran to Dani. He flung one arm around Dani's leg and wrapped the other around Chase's. "I hungry! Daddy, will you feed me more bugs?"

"You bet. I've got some big, fat ones picked out just for you." Chase lifted his gaze to Dani. His eyes turned from soft and smiling to hard and cool in an instant. "Drew, at least, knows we're already connected, no matter what you want to believe." He reached down to lift Drew into his arms, kissing his round cheek before settling the child against his shoulder like he'd been doing it fo rever.

The image of father and son, of their brown eyes and thick dark hair so like the other, along with the tender expressions on his parents' faces, gave Dani another pang of guilt. But she reminded herself she hadn't really robbed all of them of two and a half years of togetherness. Chase and his parents would have been living who knew where in the world without her and Drew anyway.

"Whatever Spud made, it'll be good," Chase

said, his head tipped against Drew's for a moment before he looked at his parents. "Then we'll make a plan for the rest of your visit with your grandson."

CHAPTER SIX

"To think you've always hassled me about my smooth moves when you're the true master," Trent said as he and Chase pulled off their gloves and gowns after surgery and headed toward the hospital corridor.

"What smooth moves?"

"Getting your parents to come and gush over Drew and put the pressure on Dani. Brilliant." Trent grinned. "Except, of course, that my moves work and yours are a pathetic failure."

"Glad you think it's funny," Chase said, still stunned at his parents' reaction to Dani not wanting to marry him. He'd been so sure his mother would have seemed, at the very least, disappointed. And with Dani's eyes looking so soft and tender as she'd watched them with Drew, he had been positive a little pressure from them would have been a big help toward his goal.

"I still can't believe they didn't back me up. Even threw me under the bus completely when they said it was between the two of us and didn't care whether we got married or not."

"I never thought I'd hear you say you wished you had more interference from outside forces in your life." Trent chuckled. "Seems to me you always complain when anybody at GPC sticks their nose in your business."

"Interference wasn't what I had in mind. Coercion was what I had in mind. Helping Dani see what's obviously the best solution here." No, the interference he was worried about might come in the form of a jerk named Matt he didn't even know. Except the guy was halfway across the world, while he had Dani with him, and there was some old saying about possession being nine-tenths of the law. He planned to take full advantage of it.

"You have no clue about women," Trent said, shaking his head. "The harder you push, the faster she'll run. Show her what a great dad you'll be to Drew and give her time."

"There might not be much time. Who knows how soon you and I'll be relocated?"

"True. But you've got to relax a little instead of bugging her to death. Let her remember why you two were together in the first place. Lord knows, I can't figure out why, but a lot of women do like you."

"I'm just trying to remind her what we had before." Seemed to have worked, for a moment at least, both times he'd kissed her. Just thinking of the feel of her mouth on his, her sweet body pressed close, made his body start to react all over again.

"Then lay off and play hard to get. I guarantee she'll start thinking of your old times in Honduras and come back for more. Women are perverse like that."

"I'm beginning to see why your relationships with women last a nanosecond." Part of Chase wanted to laugh, but Trent's words did make him pause. Could giving Dani a day or two to take the lead be the answer to speeding things up? Just the thought of heading to his next job without his ring on her finger filled him with cold anxiety.

Especially with "Mr. Matt" waiting in the wings, four thousand miles away or not.

"Trust me. She won't be able to figure out why you're suddenly not touching her and annoying her all the time. It'll drive her crazy and she'll want to jump your bones. Then she'll say yes, and you can get married." He slapped Chase's shoulder and grinned. "We'll get three weeks off before we start our new jobs. Plenty of time for a honeymoon. I bet your parents would love to have Drew stay with them up in Senegal while you and Dani go somewhere alone. You'd better start deciding where."

The thought of a week or two alone with Dani shortened Chase's breath and sent his thoughts down the erotic path they persisted in going. Not good, because he and Trent had just entered the hospital to do rounds on patients.

A halo of curly blonde hair immediately caught his attention. Dani moved her stethoscope here and there on a child's chest, and while he couldn't really see her expression, he knew it would be intent and focused.

As though she could feel him looking at her,

heart-stopping blue eyes lifted to him, and for a moment they stared at one another across the room. She seemed so far away and yet not, as though they were touching one another, breathing one another's breaths, sharing one another's thoughts, despite the expanse between them.

Trent leaned closer and in an undertone said, "Yeah, she's crazy about you. Take my advice, and I'll call the preacher." With an unholy grin he headed towards one of his patients.

Chase inhaled a deep, mind-clearing breath. Why not give Trent's method a try? What he'd been doing the past few days hadn't seemed to convince her, that was for damned sure.

He joined Dani as she checked on her patient to find out what she thought of the child's condition. She smiled at the boy before turning to Chase. "His lungs seem to be clear today. I think it's fine for him to go home tomorrow. Will you tell him?"

The boy grinned at the good news and pumped his arms in the air victoriously. Dani joined him, smiling brightly, mirroring his fists pumps with her own as she exclaimed, "Yahoo!"

The boy laughed, and Chase marveled at her cheerful exuberance. From the very first moment he'd met her he'd noticed that whenever she walked into a room, worries cleared, people smiled, and the rise in energy seemed palpable. His own energy included.

He turned to Dani. "I'm about to check on Apollo. Want to join me?"

Her beautiful eyes smiled at him. "Yes. I was waiting for you."

He liked the sound of that. More than liked it, and wished it was true in more ways than for work. Like in her room at night. In her life, for ever.

It was all he could do not to clasp her face between his palms and give her a soft kiss. He turned away and walked toward Apollo's bed.

The boy's mother had gone somewhere for the moment, with the blankets she used as she slept on the floor carefully folded and stacked. Apollo looked uncomfortable with the apparatus holding his leg in traction to keep the bones aligned, and his expression reflected his misery. He touched the child's forehead with the backs of his fingers, and it felt thankfully cool. No fever was a good sign.

"Does your leg hurt?" he asked. They'd kept him on painkillers, but sometimes it just wasn't enough. "Is the traction rubbing against you anywhere?"

The child shook his head then turned his attention to Dani as she stopped at the other side of the bed. And who could blame him for wanting to look at her? He himself could look at her all day and night, and never tire of her sweet face and vivacious smile.

"The nurses tell me he's eating and drinking okay, so that's good," Dani said to Chase. She examined the stitches in Apollo's forehead closely, then put her stethoscope in her ears and pressed the bell of it to his chest.

Chase studied the pin he'd placed in the bone as it protruded from the boy's skin. Thank God it wasn't bleeding and didn't show signs of infection. The boy was lucky. "Your leg looks good. Pretty soon we'll change the cast to cover your whole leg, okay?"

Apollo nodded, still looking miserable, poor

kid. Chase wished he could hurry the process, but controlling the pain was the best he could do for now.

"Vous avez...un coeur...très fort," Dani said haltingly to Apollo.

Chase had to grin at her accent, which was pretty bad, but he gave her credit for trying. "She's right," he said in Fon, in case the boy wasn't adept at French. "You do have a very strong heart. And your leg will be strong again, too. I promise."

"You'll be getting better every day, and that should make you smile." Dani placed her fingers gently on the corners of Apollo's mouth and tipped them up, and he gave her a small, real smile in response. "Maybe we need to find a way to help you remember that smiling and laughing will make you heal even faster."

She picked up the homemade fly swatter fan, composed of a dowel rod with cardboard taped to it. She pulled a marker from her pocket and drew a smiley face on it before turning it to fan Apollo.

"Don't worry, be happy," she began to sing in

her sweet voice. And then, in typical Dani style, she began cutely bobbing from side to side, smiling her dazzling smile.

"Don't worry, be happy." She waved the smiley-face fan and twirled around. Between singing, she coaxed, "Come on, sing with me! Don't worry, be happy."

The child attempted a feeble version of the song then laughed for the first time that day, looking starstruck.

Probably the same expression he wore when he was around her, Chase thought. He watched her slim figure dance around, looked at the sparkling blue of her eyes, and thought about the moment he'd first met her. How she'd stopped him in his tracks for a second look. And a third. Gorgeous and adorable didn't begin to cover the impact she made on everyone the second she walked in a room with that blinding smile.

At that moment Apollo's mother arrived, and beamed at Dani and her dancing and singing. Chase reassured her on the boy's progress, and Apollo turned to his mother, looking much more cheerful than when they'd first examined him.

The child spoke to her in Fon, and she smiled and nodded, looking warmly at Dani and thanking her.

"What did he say?" Dani asked.

"He says he likes the pretty doctor. But that's no surprise." He wanted to say how much he liked the pretty doctor too, but remembered he was supposed to be playing hard to get. Though that seemed kind of stupid, like he was in middle school. But he was going to give it a try, damn it.

Dani turned a bit pink. "Tell him I like him too. And that I'm glad he's starting to feel better."

After Chase did as she asked, she handed the fan to Apollo, patted his shoulder and moved to their next patient. Chase followed and focused on being all business. Just a colleague, not her former lover. Not the man who wanted to marry her and become her current lover as soon as possible. When they finished rounds, they headed back to the housing compound.

"Is it okay with you if I spend some time with Drew and my parents before we hand him back to you tonight?"

She looked surprised. "I... Sure. You don't want me there, too?"

He shrugged nonchalantly, proud of his acting skills. Yes, he wanted her there but, no, he wouldn't show it. "I just figured you'd like some time to yourself for a change. We'll play with him for a while then bring him in for dinner. Sound okay?"

"Sure," she said again, a slight frown on her face.

Cautious optimism bloomed at the confusion on her face as she clearly wondered why he wasn't touching and teasing her as he had been before. Damn it, maybe he *had* let his worry and frustration push him to come on too strongly.

Maybe Trent's idea was a good one after all.

CHAPTER SEVEN

"GOT EVERYTHING?" CHASE asked.

"I think so." Mentally, she reviewed her supply list as she looked inside her backpack. Vaccines, syringes, antibiotics, blood-sugar monitor. "Did you say there's a blood-pressure cuff already there?"

"Yeah. We keep a lockbox in the building with various things in it. Otoscope, flashlight, and a small pharmacy for drugs that don't need to be refrigerated." He threw the strap of his battered doctor's bag over his shoulder, lifted up a small box that held more of the supplies Dani carried in her backpack and headed out the door of the clinic.

She followed, refusing to notice his flexing triceps and wide, strong shoulders beneath the white polo shirt he wore. The sky was an iron gray but even without the scorching sun the air rested hot and heavy against her skin.

"You don't think it will be too much for your parents to watch Drew all day? Maybe Ruth should come give them a break."

"Are you kidding?" Chase rolled a dusty motorcycle from beneath an overhang. "They were practically rubbing their hands together with glee at the prospect of having him to themselves."

"All right, then, I won't worry. Though you already know that when he's on the go, he's like a rubber-band-powered balsa-wood plane. He keeps going until he conks out."

"Yeah. He's a lot of fun."

The indulgent smile on his face was filled with pride. Why had he been so adamant he didn't want children? It was so obvious he already adored their little boy.

"I'm sorry about having to ride the motorcycle," Chase said. He slipped the box into a bigger container attached to the bike. "I usually go alone, and didn't think to talk to Spud about the car. Didn't know he needed to get supplies today."

"In case you don't remember, we rode all over

Honduras on a bike like this." As soon as she'd said it, she wished she hadn't. Memories of Honduras weren't something she wanted to think about. Memories of her body pressed against his as they'd ridden to an off-site clinic like they were today, or when they'd had a day off to spend together and find a great hiking spot. A great lovemaking spot.

Dani shook her head to dispel the thoughts. It should be easy to forget how close they'd been back then. For some reason Chase had stopped the constant touching and teasing and tiny stolen kisses he'd been assailing her with. Surely he didn't really think she'd report him for sexual harassment?

Chase swung his leg over the bike's seat and curled his fingers around the handlebar grips, turning to look at her. "This village is only about a half-hour ride. But I warn you," he said, his teeth showing white in his smile, "the road can be rough at times. So hang on tight."

"Got it." Sitting on the back of the bike, she slipped her arms around him, her fingers curling into his taut middle.

"Ready?"

"Ready." Actually, she wasn't ready at all. Not ready for the feel of her breasts pressed against his hard body. The sensual feel of her groin pressed against his backside. The clean, masculine scent of his neck filling her nostrils.

He opened the throttle and the motorcycle took off down the dirt road. Soon there was nothing visible but groves of trees here and there and lining the bumpy road, the occasional car or truck passing them, and scooters and motorcycles often carrying as many as four and even five people. Bumps in the hard earth jammed her body against Chase and she threaded her fingers together against his sternum to keep from bouncing right off.

"You okay?" Chase shouted over the engine, glancing over his shoulder at her.

"Yes." Except for that urge she kept feeling to slip her hands beneath his shirt to feel the smooth skin she knew was right there, like she'd used to. The urge to touch more private parts as she had in Honduras when they'd been riding together, making Chase laugh and accuse her of trying to make him crash the bike. Then quickly finding the best place to enjoy finishing what she'd started.

Her own body part that she currently had pressed hard against Chase's rear began to tingle at the memories and she wished she could loosen her grip on Chase's middle to smack herself.

She had to stop thinking about their past and focus on the future. On her job. She was here to work and now to establish the framework they'd agree on regarding Drew. A second broken heart over Chase she didn't need, and the future he envisioned for them would mean exactly that.

Finally, the wide and desolate savannah showed signs of habitation. Small rectangular structures made of mud-baked walls, some with thatched roofs and others covered with corrugated steel, were scattered here and there. Happy, smiling children, many naked or wearing only colorful bottoms and beaded jewelry, played in the dirt or worked with their mothers, hanging laundry or grinding some kind of food in large vessels. A group of men and boys, their hands covered in wet, orange mud, were building a new house.

As she and Chase rode by, the men waved and shouted, grinning with pride at their work.

Chase stopped the bike next to a small, worn, cinder-block building with an open doorway and windows. When he turned off the engine, the sudden silence was a relief, with the sound of the breeze in the trees and children laughing the only things to be heard.

Dani slipped off the bike and Chase followed. "Did GPC have this place built for a clinic?" she asked.

"No. I'm told some other group built it to be a school but had to abandon the project. We use it on the first of each month so folks who aren't from this village will know when we're coming, too."

An odd stack of stones and other things atop what looked like a mud sculpture caught her eye. Nestled beneath a nearby tree, there were chains and beaded necklaces looped around the entire thing. "What's that?" she asked, pointing.

"A fetish. It's like a talisman. Voodoo to keep away bad spirits."

"Really?" She walked closer to examine it. "Does all this stuff have a special meaning?"

"I don't know about that one in particular, but it's animism. Belief that everyday objects have souls that will help and protect you."

"Do their beliefs make it hard to get people to come to the clinic, if they think the voodoo will keep them healthy and safe?"

"Sometimes. Like anywhere, it depends on the person." Chase pulled the supply box from the motorcycle and stepped towards the door. "About two hundred people live in this village, and we get quite a few from elsewhere. I think they appreciate knowing we'll be here, and rely on modern medicine more than they used to because of it. Which makes it worthwhile to come."

Dani followed him into the little building, the darkness taking a minute to get used to after the comparatively bright daylight. The single room was certainly sparsely furnished, with only a rickety-looking examination cot, a small table, and a few old chairs inside.

"So they don't use voodoo to treat illnesses?"

"They do. Sakpata is the Vodun god for illness

and healing, and many call on him and offer sacrifices when someone is sick. Priests also use healing herbs." He organized the supplies on the little table. "Vodun is an official religion in Benin, and a lot of people who are Christian or Muslim still use voodoo elements in their lives, especially when somebody's sick."

"So are you going to have someone make a little doll of me and stick it with pins to make me marry you?" She meant it as a joke, but then had to ask herself why she'd brought up the subject of marriage when he hadn't mentioned it all day.

"Don't I wish there was some way to make you agree to marry me." His lips twisted into a rueful smile. "Unfortunately, the dolls and pins thing is mostly Hollywood. While there is some black magic, it's not a significant part of voodoo. It's really about belief in ancestry and calling on the spirits to help with their lives. Peace and prosperity."

"Well, shoot, that's too bad. I was just thinking about the list of people I might want dolls made of."

"Sorry. Except not really, because I'm probably on your list." Chase stepped over to the locked box and pulled out a stethoscope, blood-pressure cuff, and some drugs to bring back to the table. "You'd be amazed by some of the fetishes, though. Hippo's feet and pig genitalia and even dog and monkey heads." He grinned. "In bigger towns there are voodoo festivals worth seeing. Drew would probably like all the colorful clothes and dancing."

"I bet he would. Maybe we could find a day to go to one." She smiled then looked out the door. Nobody seemed to be heading their way. "So now what? Do you go round people up and bring them in?"

"Round them up?" He smacked his palm against his forehead. "Darn, I forgot my lasso."

"You know what I mean." She placed her hand on his thick shoulder and gave him a little shove. "Let them know we're here."

Her vision had become used to the low light, and she could see the curve of his lips and the little crinkles in the corners of his eyes before he gave a low laugh.

"I'm sure they saw us." He reached out to tuck

loose strands of her hair behind her ears, of which there were many after their ride. As he curled one strand around his finger, his smile faded, replaced by something in his gaze that sent her heart thumping. "No way they could miss the beautiful blonde as she rode into town."

His finger travelled down her jaw and she found herself standing motionless, staring into his eyes, holding her breath. His hand dropped to his side and he turned away to briskly finish organizing the supplies.

"As people arrive, you can take care of the children and I'll look at the adults. I'll translate when you need me to. I have the records for the kids we've immunized here since I've been in Benin."

The shift in his demeanor was startling. What had happened to the Chase of yesterday who doubtless would have taken advantage of them being alone and kissed her breathless? Or, at the very least, continued with the flirting he was so good at?

She'd been sure she didn't want that from him. But when he'd turned away, suddenly all business, the traitorous part of her that had been thinking about sex during their entire motorcycle ride wanted to grab him and kiss him instead. Wanted to feel that silky skin covering hard muscle she'd been itching to touch the whole time her arms had been wrapped around him.

She mentally thrashed herself and pulled her own supplies from the backpack. Apparently her libido, which had come to life since seeing him again, wasn't up on the fact that her sensible brain wanted to keep their relationship platonic.

As if by voodoo, the first patients suddenly appeared at the doorway and the next hours were filled with basic examinations and immunizations, distribution of drugs for various problems, medicine to rid children of intestinal worms— which were apparently common here, as they had been in Honduras—and topical or oral antibiotics for the occasional infected wound.

Communicating with the children and their parents was surprisingly easy, with hand gestures working pretty well and Chase translating over his shoulder for the rest.

After being concerned at first that they'd have few patients, Dani couldn't believe the line of children, standing three and four deep, waiting for their shots. After being so frustrated at the sorry state of the immunization records they had, she was more than pleased at how much she'd be able to add to the database after today.

What a great feeling to know that coming here could make such a difference in the health of these kids. More than once during the day she smiled at Chase and his return smile was filled with a sense of connection, the same understanding of exactly what each was feeling that they'd shared long ago.

By late in the afternoon the line had dwindled to just a few stragglers. The work left Dani feeling both tired and energized at their accomplishments.

"How long do you usually stay?" she asked Chase as she cleaned her hands with antiseptic and looked at the few people remaining outside. "Do you hang around until there's nobody waiting?"

"It depends. Obviously, at some point you just need to shut it down, especially when it gets dark early. Believe me, you don't want to be riding home on a motorcycle after the sun sets. It's not common to be robbed, but it does happen." He grinned at her. "And the last time I rode on all those rough potholes without being able to see, I was more convinced I might not live another day than the time I walked across a frayed rope bridge over the Amazon in a windstorm."

Now, there was a image. Dani laughed. "Then let's be sure to wrap it up before then. We don't want to orphan Drew."

The thought squashed her amusement. In her will she'd listed her own mother as guardian to Drew if anything ever happened to her. But her mother was alone, and tremendously busy. Now that Chase was involved in Drew's life, should they make other arrangements?

"You know, we should talk about that, unlikely as it is, as we figure out our future arrangements with regard to Drew," she said. "If something happened to me, I figured my mother should take him. But maybe your parents would be a better choice."

Chase's expression turned fierce. "No. That's

not a good option. Nothing's going to happen to us."

"But we—"

Distraught shouting interrupted her thought as a man pushed his way through the few people standing in line and burst through the doorway.

CHAPTER EIGHT

CHASE STEPPED OVER to him, speaking in an authoritative yet calming voice that seemed to help the man get himself under control. Dani wished she knew what was going on, but it was clearly something that would need their attention. The man spoke fast with frantic gestures, and the frown and concern on Chase's face grew more pronounced.

Chase spoke to Dani as he shoved some items in his medical bag and flung the strap over his shoulder. "I need to go with him. He lives about half a mile away, so I'm going to take the bike to get there fast. I'll tell the last in line we'll come back next week so you can put stuff away and lock up the drugs as quickly as possible. Someone can show you where I am. You'll have to walk, but I think I might need you there."

"What's wrong?"

"His wife's in labor and something's not right. She's bleeding and in abnormal, extereme pain— the midwife doesn't know what to do. Assuming we have a live infant, your expertise may help."

He spoke quickly to a man in line, who nodded. "This man will show you where she is."

"Okay." She'd barely uttered the words before Chase left with the worried husband, and the sound of the motorcycle engine came to her just moments later.

Dani quickly stashed the medical supplies and pharmaceuticals in the lock box then followed the man Chase had asked to guide her through the village.

A rusty bike leaned against the wall of the clinic building and to her surprise he gestured for her to get on it. While it would be great to get there faster than it would take to walk, it wouldn't help to ride it if she had no idea where she was going.

The man cleared up that question when he straddled the bike himself while still gesturing for her to get on the battered seat. Precariously perching herself on it, she placed her hands on the man's shoulders and he pedaled off.

At first their wobbling movement was so slow she ground her teeth in frustration. They'd never get there at this rate, and an increasingly disturbing feeling fluttered in her stomach that the situation just might be dire.

Thankfully, the guy seemed to get the hang of pedaling standing up with her weight behind him, as they picked up speed on the bumpy dirt path, passing a hodgepodge of straw huts and mud houses.

The sound of a woman's moans and cries made the skin over her skull tighten and the bike stopped outside a hut that seemed larger than several others nearby.

She jumped off the bike. "Chase?"

"In here."

She followed his grim voice and stopped just inside the doorway, stunned at the scene. The writhing and moaning woman in labor lay on a pad on the floor that had at one time been some yellowish color but was now stained red with the blood that was literally everywhere. All over the poor woman's lower body. The dirt floor. The midwife, crouched beside her and holding her hand. Chase.

"What's wrong?" Her heart tripped in her chest. "What can I do?"

"Placental abruption. You can see the pain she's in, and her abdomen is rock-hard." He finished swabbing the woman's belly with antiseptic wipes and drew some drug into a needle. "Got to do an emergency C-section. I'm about to give her a local anesthetic, which is the best I can do here. Then we've got to get that baby out."

She crouched next to him. "Tell me what to do."

"Get my knife out of my bag. The ball suction to clear the baby's mouth and nose. The ambu-bag. Then get ready, because when I pull the baby out I'm handing it to you and praying like hell."

She grabbed the bag and went through its contents to find what he needed. She snapped on a pair of gloves and grabbed some antiseptic wipes to clean the knife.

Chase injected the woman's stomach in multiple locations until there was nothing left in the syringe, then tossed it aside to take the knife from Dani.

"Are you going to do a low, transverse incision?" She had a feeling the usual C-section standard wouldn't apply here in this hut, with the poor woman likely bleeding to death.

"No. We'll be damned lucky if a vertical gets the baby out in time."

With a steady hand Chase made a single, smooth slice through the skin beginning at the woman's umbilicus down to her pelvis, exposing the hard, enlarged uterus within the cavity. Chase looked briefly at Dani, his jaw tense. "Ready?"

She nodded and prepared herself for fast action. Adrenaline surged through her veins as she knew the infant had probably lost its oxygen connection to its mother and would need immediate help to breathe on its own. If it was still alive.

Chase began the second incision through the uterus itself, exposing the infant. He reached into the womb and carefully lifted the baby out, using his fingers to wipe the baby boy's tiny face and body gently to remove the tangle of clotted-off blood vessels that had torn and lead to the abruption.

"Here." He passed the motionless baby to Dani and began scooping out the loosened placenta from the mother's uterus. "I've got to get her bleeding stopped or we'll lose her."

The infant was dark purple, his lips nearly black from lack of oxygen. Dani quickly used the bulb suction to clear the amniotic fluid, mucus, and black meconium from his mouth, nose, and throat, but he still didn't breathe.

Heart pounding, she attached the smallest mask to the ambu-bag then placed the mask over the baby's nose and mouth. She slowly and evenly squeezed the bulb, praying the air would inflate the baby's lungs.

After what seemed an eternity a shudder finally shook his tiny body. He coughed and drew in several gasping breaths before weakly crying out. His little arms and legs started jerking around and as his cries grew stronger, Dani sagged with relief.

She grabbed one of the stacked cloths the midwife must have put by the mother and quickly wiped the baby down. Getting him dryer and warmer was critical to keeping him from going into shock.

Satisfied that he was now warm enough, she grasped the umbilical cord and milked it gently, trying to get every drop of the cord blood into the baby's body. She then cut the cord and clamped it off.

Looking into the baby's little face, she saw he was no longer crying, his eyes wide as he saw the world for the first time, and it filled her heart with elation. "We did it! We did it!" she said, turning to Chase.

"Good. Give him to the midwife and get me another clamp."

His tone and expression were tight, controlled as he worked to sew the woman's uterus, and Dani's jubilation faded as she switched her focus from the infant to his mother.

The woman was speaking between moans, looking at her baby, but blood still flowed from her body. Such a frightening quantity that Dani knew they had very little time.

She quickly stood to pass the baby to the midwife then grabbed a clamp from his bag. She kneeled next to him again, heart racing. Why was the woman still bleeding? It looked like he'd already tied off the big uterine veins and stitched the uterus itself.

"What's wrong, Chase?"

He shook his head. "Uterus can't seem to naturally clamp down and stop the flow. Check her pulse."

Dani pressed her fingers to the woman's wrist and stared at her watch. "One-forty," she said, dismayed. Clearly, the woman's pulse was rocketing to compensate for her blood volume loss.

He worked several more minutes in silence. "Damn it!" Fiercely intense, he turned to look at Dani. "Get me the garbage bag that's in the motorcycle box and the sponges and gauze in there. Hurry."

She ran to grab what he asked for, wondering what he could possibly have planned but not about to ask with the situation so dire. As she hurried back into the hut she heard him barking orders and the few other women in the room ran off.

Blood literally dripping from his hands and arms, he grimly took the garbage bag from Dani. He slipped his hands inside the bag and began to ease it into the woman's belly cavity.

"What in the world are you doing?" In her astonishment the question just burst from her lips.

"Packing the belly. Like a big internal bandage. It's her only chance. I'll stuff it with the sponges and strips of cloth the women are getting. Tamp it down and apply pressure to stop the bleeding. Pray like hell."

He grabbed the sponges and gauze and stuffed them inside the garbage bag. Then he yanked off his own bloody shirt and rapidly tore it into small strips before stuffing them, too, into the bag. The women returned with cloth strips and he shoved them inside before pressing on it all with his hands.

He kept the pressure on the woman's belly for long minutes before lifting his gaze to Dani. With blood spattered across his face and naked torso, his eyes looked harshly intense. "Check her vitals again."

She quickly took the woman's pulse, and her heart tripped. "One-fifteen. It's working!"

She doubted they'd get it down to a normal reading of seventy, but at least it was heading in the right direction.

"Call Spud. Tell him to get a car here stat to take her to our hospital. We can't transfuse there, but if we pump her with fluids, it should be enough."

She stepped outside the hut to call Spud, and when she returned she saw that Chase was stitching the woman's belly closed with the filled garbage bag still inside.

"So, you leave it in there until she clots well enough? Then take it out?" Dani had never seen such a thing. Never even heard of it. Amazement and awe swept through her at Chase's incredible knowledge and skill.

"Belly-packing is battlefield medicine." He continued his steady, even stitches to completely close the incision except for the very top of the garbage bag, which was still exposed. The plastic extended outside the woman's body as he stitched around it. "Eventually, we'll be able to pull the sponges and cloth out piece by piece, then the empty bag, and hopefully not have to open her up again."

The woman started speaking again in barely a whisper. In spite of what she'd been through, she extended her arms towards the midwife. Holding her new, tiny son close to her breast, she kissed his head and managed a weak smile.

Dani's throat filled and tears stung her eyes. Chase had done this. He'd somehow, miraculously, saved this woman's life. Her baby hadn't lost his mother.

Chase spoke to the women who'd fetched the strips of cloth, and they brought several pads and put them beneath the patient's legs. Obviously, Chase was concerned about her going into shock before they got her to the hospital.

The women brought some water and, silently, Chase stripped off his gloves and washed the blood off his chest and arms as best he could, with Dani following suit. Spud arrived with a nurse from the hospital, and they carried the woman and her baby to the car and drove off.

Other than quick instructions to Spud and the

nurse, Chase had barely spoken for fifteen minutes. Standing next to the motorcycle after they'd packed everything up, Dani touched his arm.

"That was amazing. I've never seen anything like it. You should be very proud of what you did today."

He didn't respond, just looked at her. She couldn't decipher the emotion on his face exactly but it definitely wasn't triumph, which was what she thought he'd be feeling. It seemed more like despair.

He reached for her, grasping her shoulders, and slowly pulled her against his bare chest, which was still sprinkled with dried blood. His lips touched her forehead, lingered, until he stepped back to mount the bike.

Chase was quiet the entire ride back to the GPC compound. Not that there could be much conversation over the loud engine, but on the way to the village he'd managed to throw the occasional comment or observation over his shoulder. Probably the low light made it even more important that he concentrate on avoiding precarious ruts and potholes.

This time her arms were wrapped around a naked torso, and she had to control the constant urge to press her palms to his skin, slide them across the soft hair on his chest, down to the hard corrugated muscle of his stomach. Distracting him while driving in the near dark was definitely not a good idea.

After they'd unpacked the items they hadn't used and returned them to the clinic, Chase seemed remote, preoccupied. "I'm going to go clean up. See you and Drew at dinner."

"Okay." She didn't know what to think of his demeanor. Distance. The lack of touching and flirting earlier that day. And for the past forty-five minutes he'd spoken to her as though they were strangers.

Annoyed with herself at the hurt she felt because of the sudden change in him, she decided to check on Drew before she, too, washed off all the road dirt and changed her bloody clothes. She knew the Bowens had Drew, but had no idea exactly where they were. She turned to find out and felt a hand close over her forearm.

"Do you have pictures of Drew when he was first born? When he was a baby?"

"Of course. Though I don't know how many I have with me. Some on my laptop and a few on my phone."

"I'd like to see them."

Why did he appear so oddly somber? How could he not be elated that fate had sent them to the village that day? "You know, you did just save two lives today. I'm surprised you aren't exhilarated." She certainly had been, until his seriousness had tempered it.

"We saved their lives together." He placed his hand on her cheek. "And three years ago we made a life together."

His eyes were now darkly intense, and she tried to decipher the jumble of emotions there, all mixed up with his somber demeanor and the grim lines around his mouth. He almost looked... Could the word be vulnerable? She searched his face and realized, stunned, that was exactly the word. Never would she have guessed the *über*-talented, ultra-confident Chase Bowen could ever look or feel vulnerable in any way. No matter what the circumstances, he always seemed…invincible.

"Yes, we did," Dani said softly. "And I can see you're as proud of him as I am. I'll find what photos I can and show them to you after dinner."

He nodded and turned to walk to his room, leaving her staring at his back and asking herself if she really knew him as well as she thought she did.

She went to find Drew, and had to wonder. In her infatuation with Chase, with his obvious strengths that had dazzled her so, had she never taken time to look inside at the rest of the man? At all facets of him and his life and what had shaped him to become the person he was today?

Chase was her son's father. They might not be spending much time together in the future, but the emotion on Chase's face tonight proved she needed to understand better what made the man tick.

CHAPTER NINE

CHASE LAY ON his bed, his hair still wet from his shower, and stared at the cracked ceiling. He hoped everyone went ahead and started dinner—he and Dani had arrived back much later than they'd expected as it was. But he needed a few more minutes to deal with the overwhelming feelings that had unexpectedly swamped him after the birth of the baby that afternoon.

Damn it, he'd never wanted this. Never wanted to be susceptible to the same kind of pain he'd felt when his brother had died. Never wanted to feel vulnerable to his whole universe being crushed in an instant.

But when he'd brought that baby into the world, the moment had taken away his breath.

In his career he'd delivered more babies than he could possibly guess at. Had always appreciated the miracle of birth, the joy of the mother, the pride of the father. Had enjoyed gently passing a healthy infant to suckle at its mother's breast, and sympathized with the loss when a baby hadn't made it.

Never had it felt personal. Until today. The first baby he'd delivered since he'd found out he had a child of his own. Seeing the baby's tiny body, hearing his first cries, watching him looking with wide eyes at the world for the very first time had clutched at his heart like nothing before.

And the mother. She'd suffered so much with the baby's birth and yet, barely escaping death and in tremendous pain, she'd smiled through it all when she'd first seen her son.

He'd missed that with Drew. Missed being there to help Dani. And he hated that he'd never even thought to ask her if it had been an easy birth or a hard one. Even with all the modern technology in the U.S., not all babies were born without complications.

He scrubbed his hands over his face. He never wanted to feel the cold terror for Dani and Drew that had gripped him as he'd worked with mother and infant today. The sudden fear that if something happened to either of them, his entire world would be ripped to pieces. How did people cope with that? Did they just refuse to see the dangers? The risks?

Inhaling a shaky breath, he swung his legs off the bed and sat up. The past couldn't be changed. Andrew had been conceived and born healthy and he was the most beautiful child Chase had ever seen. And Dani was a very special woman. An incredible woman.

He'd do whatever he had to do to keep both of them safe.

As he stepped through the doorway of the kitchen, it looked like everyone had finished eating but Dani. The scene was much livelier than usual, the room filled with Spud, Trent, Dani, his parents, and Drew, who obviously enjoyed being the center of everyone's attention. Laughter at his antics bounced off the walls of the room, but Dani's big smile faded as he walked in, her blue gaze seeming contemplative.

He hoped like hell she hadn't sensed how disturbed he'd felt. He also hoped he had all those feelings under control.

"Daddy!" Drew grinned and raised his arms toward Chase, his fingers gooey with mashed yams.

Chase's chest felt peculiarly heavy and light at the same time. He couldn't believe how quickly Drew had accepted him as his dad. How he wanted to be held by him. To be played with by him. He had to swallow hard to shove down the emotions that had swamped him earlier.

"Hey, lizard-boy. What have you been up to today?" He grabbed a wet towel, partly to give himself something to do, and wiped Drew's hands before sitting next to him.

"Your mother and I showed him the technique for shinnying up a palm tree today," Phil said. "He's a natural. Even better than you when you were that age."

"Yes," Evelyn agreed with a proud smile. "He made it up at least three feet. With us spotting, of course. Pretty soon he'll be getting all the way up to grab a coconut or two."

"Little did I know this was a Bowen family tradition," Dani said with a smile. "When Chase first showed off how he could climb a coconut tree, I thought it was just a macho thing he did to impress women."

"It worked, didn't it?" Chase asked. He conjured up a smile and took a swallow of beer, hoping it would help him relax and feel more normal. Last thing he wanted was to have anyone guess at his feelings. Or, worse, ask.

"A few of the places we lived actually had palm-tree climbing contests. Chase and his brother even won occasionally," his mother said.

Chase stiffened and glanced at Dani. He'd never mentioned Brady to her. Or to Trent or Spud, for that matter. What were the chances they wouldn't ask questions?

"Chase has a brother?" Dani looked questioningly from his mother to him, her eyebrows raised.

Obviously, no chance. Chase gritted his teeth. The last thing he wanted to talk about was Brady. Not ever and especially not today.

"Had." Evelyn's eyes shadowed. "He—"

"Dani said she'd find some pictures of Andrew when he was a baby," Chase interrupted. He wasn't hungry anyway, and stood to gather empty plates, with Spud following suit. "I know you two proud grandparents want to see them as much as I do."

Dani looked at him for a long moment before speaking. "Yes. I had more downloaded than I realized."

She stood to retrieve her computer from a kitchen shelf, and Chase drew a deep breath of relief. Not that she wouldn't ask again, but at least he'd be prepared to give the most basic account possible, without his parents around to embellish it, before changing the subject.

Everyone crowded around as Dani gave a slide show on her laptop. Drew had been so damned cute as a baby, with a shock of dark hair sticking up around his head, his brown eyes wide, his cheeks round and pink. Sitting on the floor amid a pile of blocks, a big grin showing just a few teeth, drool dripping from the corners of his mouth like a bulldog. She even had a video of him crawling up to the hearth in her little house, pulling himself to his feet then yanking to the floor the houseplant perched there, scattering dirt everywhere.

It was a hell of a thing that he'd missed it all.

Amid the laughing and *aww*s echoing in the kitchen, and Drew's delight at his photos, Chase found himself looking at Dani between nearly every picture. The love and tenderness in her eyes as she looked at the captured moments in time. Not so very different from the expression on her enchanting face when they'd shared so many intimate moments in Honduras.

Her smiling gaze met his more than once, warm and close, and he almost blurted out the words right there in front of everyone. Almost asked why she was being so stubborn about marrying him when they had this beautiful child between them. The closeness they'd shared before and could share again. Why? Did she still honestly not believe him, or trust him, when he promised they could make it work? Was it her feelings for that Matt guy?

"That's it, I'm afraid." Dani shut her laptop with a smile at Drew. "I need to remember to take more pictures while we're here in Benin. You seem to grow bigger every day."

"The good news there is that Drew has grandparents with a very nice camera who now have a new favorite subject," Phil said. "We've taken so many of him it's a good thing I brought an extra memory card. Too bad we have to leave in a couple days."

"Perhaps you and Dani can bring Drew to Senegal," Evelyn said to Chase. "How much longer are you here in Benin?"

"Not sure." He wasn't about to go into that potential problem right now. He didn't know if Dani knew he'd be leaving soon, and the last thing he wanted to give her was another reason to think they shouldn't make things permanent between them.

Drew yawned, and Chase grabbed the excuse to get out of there. "Looks like a certain tree-climbing monkey needs to go to bed," he said, lifting him into his arms. Drew snaked his arms around Chase's neck and he held the child's little body close. Would he ever stop feeling the amazement, the joy that nearly hurt at having this little guy in his life?

"I a lizard, not a monkey," Drew said with another yawn.

His eyelids drooped and Chase headed for the door then stopped to look at Dani. He realized he didn't know Drew's bedtime routine, and that had to change. "You coming?"

She nodded, saying her goodnights to everyone before following him down the hall to her room.

"I'll get him ready. You don't have to stay," Dani said as she pulled Drew's Spiderman pajamas from a drawer.

"I want to know what's involved in getting him ready for bed," Chase said. He gently sat a half-asleep Drew on the edge of the bed and took the pajamas from Dani. Afraid the child would conk out before he'd even had a chance to change him, Chase quickly pulled Drew's little striped shirt over his head and finished getting him into his PJs.

"We usually read a book after using the bathroom, but I don't think he's going to stay awake for that tonight," Dani said as she put Drew's discarded clothes away.

Together, they took him down the hall to take care of bathroom necessities before tucking him into bed.

"'Night, Daddy," he said, lifting his sweet face for a kiss.

"'Night, Drew. Sleep tight."

Drew did the same with Dani, and as Chase watched her soft lips brush their child's cheek, saw her slender fingers tuck her unruly hair behind her ears, saw her tempting round behind as she bent over, he knew he couldn't play the hard-to-get game any longer. Not just because it hadn't seemed to work, he thought wryly.

He had to touch her. Had to kiss those soft lips. Had to satisfy the desire, the longing he'd barely been able to contain since she'd first arrived. Since he'd first seen her silhouetted in the sub-Saharan twilight.

He needed her tonight, and could only hope she'd give in to the feelings he knew they'd both shared, remembered, since finding one another again. Let him show her what she meant to him. Let him show her how good their future could be.

She straightened and stepped closer to Chase in the small room. "He's already sound asleep," she said with a smile. "Your parents wore him out. Or he wore them out. They've obviously had a wonderful day. Thank you."

"For…?"

"For bringing them here. For Drew getting to know them. He hardly has any family and yours is…special."

Her luminous eyes looked up at him, held him, and he closed the gap between them. He pulled her close, hoping she wouldn't resist, object. "Not as special as you. No one is as special as you."

Then he kissed her. Slowly. Softly. Not wanting to push, to rush, to insist. He wanted her to want the same thing he wanted. For them to join together and make love in a way that made everything else fade away. All the worries, the fears he'd felt earlier buried beneath the kind of passion only she had ever inspired in him.

She tasted faintly of coffee and vitality and Dani, and she kissed him back with the same slow tenderness he gave her. So different from the spontaneous combustion of their previous kisses. The kisses he fed her, that she gave in return, were full of a quietly blossoming heat.

Slowly weakening him as they strengthened his need.

Her hands tentatively swept over his chest and shoulders to cup the back of his head, her tongue in a languid dance with his. He pulled her tightly against him, loving the feel of her soft curves molded perfectly to his body. Made for him.

She broke the kiss. "You are the most confusing man."

"Not true." He brushed her lips with his because he couldn't stand even a moment's distance. "There's nothing confusing about what I want right now."

He kissed her again, and her sigh of pleasure nearly had him forgetting about gently coaxing. Nearly had him lifting her to the bed and yanking off their clothes to tangle their bodies together, to feel every inch of her skin next to his.

She pulled her mouth away with a little gasping breath. "A couple of days ago you wouldn't stop touching and kissing me then all day today you acted like we barely knew one another."

"So it did work." He pressed his mouth below

her ear. Tasted her soft throat. Breathed in her sweet, distinctive scent.

"What worked?"

"I was playing hard to get. Trent told me to. Said you'd want to jump my bones."

She gave a breathy laugh. "I swear, boys never grow up, do they?"

"So, do you?" He slipped his hands up her ribs, let one wander higher. "Want to jump my bones?"

Her lips curved, but she shook her head. "I don't think that's a good idea. We have…issues to resolve without making things harder."

"Except something's already harder."

She chuckled, her eyes twinkling, and he knew he could look into the amazing blue of them for ever. He kissed her again, hoping to make her forget about any and all issues and just feel.

Surely she could sense, through his kiss, what she meant to him. That she wouldn't stop and pull away and end the beauty of the moment before it began. That she could feel what she did to him through the pounding of his heart and the short-ness of his breath.

Dani pulled her mouth from his and untwined

her hands from behind his neck. She stepped out of his hold, and Chase tried to control the frustration that had him wanting to grab her and refuse to let her go. "Dani—"

"Shh." She pressed her fingers to his lips then slid their warmth down his arm to grasp his hand. "Your room is close by, right? Let's go there. We'll hear Drew if he wakes up."

Relief practically weakened his knees. Or, more likely, he thought with a smile, they'd already been weakened by her. "Come on."

Dragging her behind him, Chase could hear her practically running as he strode the short distance down the hall to his room, but slowing down wasn't an option. He'd barely shut and locked the door behind them before he grabbed her again.

This time the kisses didn't start out sweet and slow. He found himself in a rush, his mouth taking hers with a fierceness and possessiveness he couldn't seem to control. His hands slid over her bottom, up her sides to her belly and breasts, further until he cradled her head. He released her ponytail, and the tangle of her hair curling around his hands took him back to the first time he'd kissed her, when those ringlets had captured his fingers and refused to let go.

"I've always loved your crazy curls," he said. "Love the way it feels, tickling my skin."

"Well, if you really love it…" Her soft fingers slipped up his ribs and he shivered as she pulled his shirt over his head. She leaned forward and nuzzled his neck, her wild hair caressing his shoulders, and he couldn't control a groan.

"I love your hair, too," she said. Her hands traveled back up his chest before she buried her fingers in his hair, pulling his mouth down to hers for a deep kiss. "It's like thick silk. Drew's lucky he has your hair and not mine."

Her lips were curved and her eyes were full of the same desire that surged through his every cell. "I can't agree," he said. "But arguing with you isn't on our agenda right now. Getting both of us naked is."

He tugged off her shirt then reached for the button on her shorts before desperation seemed to grab both of them at the same time and every garment was quickly shed until both stood naked in front of each other.

His breath caught in his throat. Three years since he'd seen her beautiful body. Three years without enjoying her small, perfect breasts. The curve of her waist, her slim hips and legs, the blonde curls covering the bliss between them. Three years without touching and tasting every inch of her soft, ivory skin, and suddenly he couldn't wait one more second to join with her.

He reached for her at the same time she reached for him, and they practically fell onto his bed with a bounce.

Her breasts grazed his chest and he dipped his head to take one pink nipple into his mouth. With his eyes closed, tasting first one taut tip then the other, he could imagine they'd been together just yesterday, without the three years of distance between them. He could hope, as his lips traveled over her flat abdomen, that she had missed him as much as he'd missed her. He could believe, as his fingers explored the moist juncture of her thighs, as he breathed in the scent of her, as he listened to her moans of pleasure, that she was already his, for ever.

"Chase." As she gasped his name, her hands tugged at his head, his arms, his torso.

He rose to lie above her and she opened her arms and body to him, a beckoning smile on her beautiful lips.

"You said your goal was to make me want to jump your bones." Her voice vibrated against his chest. "You've succeeded. So do it."

She held him close, wriggling beneath him, trying to position herself in a way that left him no option for staying strong and enjoying her body for a whole lot longer.

He managed a short laugh. "And you call me bossy." He wanted to kiss that smiling mouth of hers, but wanted to watch her, too. He slipped inside her heat, and was glad he could see her eyes, her lips. See her desire, her pleasure. Knowing he gave it to her.

He wanted, more than anything, to give her pleasure. He wanted to make this moment last, to show her he would give her everything. To assuage whatever worries she had about them staying together for ever.

As they moved, he tried to take it slowly. To draw out the distinctive rhythm the two of them had always shared. But the little sounds she kept making, the way she kissed him, the way she wrapped her legs around him and drew him in drove him out of his mind.

He couldn't last much longer. He reached between them to touch her most sensitive place as they moved together, and was rewarded as she closed her eyes and uttered his name. Saw the release on her beautiful face as he let himself fall with her.

The quiet room was filled with the sound of their breathing as they lay there, skin to skin. He buried his face in the sweetly scented spirals of her hair, stroking his hand slowly up her side to cup her soft breast.

He smiled. After what they'd just shared, even stubborn Dani couldn't deny they belonged together.

Neither seemed to want to move, and they lay there for long minutes, skin to warm skin. Until her hands shoved at his shoulders and he managed to lift himself off her and roll to one side. With his fingers splayed across her stomach, he finally caught his breath.

"If I didn't know better, I'd think I didn't have any bones left for you to jump," he said, kissing her arm.

"I have to check on Drew."

She struggled to get up and Chase swung his legs off the bed to give her room. Then, shocked, he saw the expression on her face.

It wasn't full of blissful afterglow, the way he knew his had been. It was sad and worried. Distant.

What the hell had happened?

"Dani." He reached for her hand, but she shook him off, grabbed up her clothes and quickly put them on.

"I'm sorry." Her voice was tight, controlled, so unlike the Dani he used to know as she struggled with the button on her shorts. "This was…a mistake. We shouldn't have complicated an already complicated problem."

Chase tamped down a surge of anger at her

words. "You're the one making it a complicated problem. To me, there's no problem at all."

"Our…making love…doesn't change anything. Doesn't solve the problem of you wanting us to be married and act like we're a normal family while you live halfway across the world."

"Damn it, Dani." He grasped her arm and halted her progress in getting on her shoes. "We *can* be a normal family. How many people travel on business while their spouse keeps things going at home? It's the same thing."

She pulled her arm loose and slipped on her sandals. "It's not the same thing. Do I have to keep saying it over and over? Seeing you just a few months a year, Drew would wonder why your work is more important than he is."

"I'd make sure he knows he's the most important thing in my life. That you both are." He wanted to shake her. How could she still put up this damned wall between them after what they'd just shared?

She shoved her glorious curls from her face and finally looked him in the eye. He saw the same despair and anxiety that had been there from the minute she'd arrived in Benin, and didn't know what the hell to do about it. Hadn't he given her every reason to trust him? Why could she not see what was so very clear?

He tried to reach for her, but she stepped to the door, shaking her head. "I need to check on Drew," she said again. "And I need to think. About you and me and my own mission work and Drew. I'll…see you tomorrow."

As the door clicked behind her, he nearly dropped down onto the bed in frustrated defeat.

After what they'd shared, he'd been sure he'd won her tonight. And didn't know what the hell his next move should be.

CHAPTER TEN

CHASE WALKED INTO the kitchen after his run and workout to make coffee for Dani. An extra five miles had cleared his head and brought renewed optimism. Surely, after last night, she'd dreamed of him the way he'd dreamed of her. Relived every achingly sweet moment in her arms and body.

He'd hated feeling so shaken and disturbed last night before dinner. Not a feeling he was used to, and definitely a feeling he didn't like. But making love with Dani had calmed him, soothed him, deep within his soul, and he wanted that again. And again.

Hopefully, she was over whatever had prompted her doubts and regrets and quick exit last night. And if she wasn't over it, he had a plan to get her over it.

His plan was to take a cup of coffee to her

room, awaken her with a kiss then, assuming Drew was still asleep, kiss her and touch her and convince her that a morning shower together was the perfect way to start the day. Just thinking about kissing her soft lips and soaping her every delicate curve had him breathing faster.

Maybe he should just forget about waiting for the coffee to brew and head in there that minute. Except the woman was addicted to her morning coffee, and the gesture would probably soften her up and help him get what he wanted. Her, naked, wet, and slippery against his equally naked, wet, and slippery body.

Reminded yet again of what they had together. Why they belonged together.

Despite the uncertainty of his plan, he had to chuckle, thinking about how irritated she used to get when he dragged her out of bed early in the morning to do push-ups and sit-ups with him. A cup of coffee under her nose, though, always seemed to bring down her annoyance and bring up that sunny smile that had him starting the day with a smile of his own.

Drumming his fingers against the countertop

as he listened to the coffee perk, he spotted yesterday's mail in a small pile. After being gone all day then preoccupied afterwards, he hadn't looked at it. A good distraction from his currently surging libido.

He shuffled through the envelopes then stopped cold when he spotted one addressed to him with the GPC logo and return address. The back of his neck tightened and he had a bad, bad feeling he knew what it was.

He ripped open the envelope and unfolded the letter. It didn't take more than a quick skim of its contents to see he'd been right.

Damn it! Half crumpling the letter, he pressed both palms to the countertop.

Panama. His new assignment. One more week here, three weeks off, then Central America.

What the hell should he do now?

No way was he heading to Panama before Dani became his wife. Even if he stayed here for the three weeks' vacation, she'd have plenty of work to do with the two new surgeons arriving to replace him and Trent. Unless she was willing to share her room and single bed, which she apparently wasn't ready to do, he'd have to find another place to stay. Acquire his own car or scooter to get around.

He straightened. Those were easy things to accomplish. The hard part was convincing Dani that marriage between them was best all round. The way they'd burned up the sheets last night should have shown her they still had what they'd shared in Honduras and had her saying yes right then.

Damn it to hell. Could GPC have possibly sent him farther away? It couldn't have been the Congo, or someplace close where he could fairly easily hop a plane to see her and Drew?

No, it had to be literally halfway across the world from Dani.

Without a guarantee that he could charm and cajole her into marriage before he had to leave, he couldn't afford to just hope absence would make the heart grow fonder, or however that stupid old saying went. More likely it would be out of sight, out of mind, and she'd end up back with Matt in less than eight months, leaving *him* in the cold and with no influence at all about what mission trips she might head to in the future with their son in tow.

An icy hollow formed in his chest at the thought of never again holding her or kissing her. Maybe even having to see her with some other man when he visited Drew.

No. Not happening.

Various solutions spun through his mind until he struck one that seemed viable. He'd been with GPC a long time. Year-round, unlike a lot of docs. And his parents had worked for them at least thirty years. Surely all that gave him some clout.

In a few hours, when the GPC offices opened, he'd make a phone call. Tell his old buddy Mike Hardy that Dani and her son needed a change of assignment from Benin, and to find someone to replace her. That she needed to join him in Panama for the duration of her contract commitment.

He sucked in a calming breath and nodded. Yeah. It could work. Somehow he'd get the folks at the GPC to keep mum on why she was being reassigned with him. Come up with a good reason she'd believe.

The kitchen door swung open and he jumped as he turned to see who it was.

Trent. A breath of relief whooshed from his lungs.

"What are you up to?" Trent asked, eyebrows raised. "You look like you just robbed the GPC piggy bank. Shake out your pockets so I can see if there's more than a buck fifty in there."

Thank God it wasn't Dani, because if Trent was getting guilty vibes from him, she'd be sure to suspect he was up to something. She'd always had a sixth sense when it came to what he was thinking and feeling.

"Just wondering how I can snitch that fancy watch you bought in Switzerland before you head to your next assignment." Chase threw out a grin he hoped was convincing. The last thing he wanted was another lecture from Trent on how to deal with Dani. On playing hard to get or letting things unfold as they would or whatever the hell he came up with next. "So, where are they sending you?"

"Eastern India. West Bengal, to be exact." Trent grabbed a cup and poured the coffee Chase hadn't noticed had finished brewing. "How about you?"

"Panama." Just the word made his stomach churn.

Trent sipped his coffee and gave him a measuring look. "So, now what?"

Chase didn't pretend to not know what he meant. "Not sure. I'm thinking I'll call Mike at GPC and have Dani reassigned with me."

Trent nearly spit out his coffee as he choked. "Reassigned with you?" He burst out laughing. "Oh, man, I want to be in the room when she finds out you're moving her halfway across the world without even asking."

"None of this is funny." Chase gritted his teeth. "I can't go all the way to Panama without things tied up between us. Or anywhere else, for that matter. And since it's not looking like that's going to happen in a few weeks, the logical solution is for her to come with me."

"You are so delusional." Trent shook his head. "Do you really think Dani would want to marry a guy who's so controlling that he first demands marriage and then, when she says no, manipulates the whole world so things will turn out the way he wants them to?"

"This has nothing to do with being controlling." Why the hell did everyone keep accusing him of that? "This has to do with making the best decision and getting married because of Drew."

"*Your* best decision. Which isn't necessarily *her* best decision."

"What, you think I'd be a lousy husband? Thanks a hell of a lot." Surprise and anger burned in his chest. "You know, I'm damned tired of my friends and family turning on me this way. I try to do right by my own son and all I get is a raft of crap over it." He grabbed a glass of orange juice and downed it in one gulp. "I'm calling the GPC. And once Dani and I are married and happy, there's no way she'll be mad about moving with me."

Trent looked at him steadily before he gave a small shrug. "You know her better than I do. And I honestly wish you the best of luck because, of course, I know you'd be good to her and Drew. But I think you're making a mistake if you don't talk to her first."

The sound of squeaking hinges preceded Dani as she came into the kitchen. Absently, Chase recognized the anticipation in her eyes—it was her I-smell-coffee look. Her pleased expression morphed into a frown as she looked first at Chase then at Trent then back at Chase, a question in her blue eyes.

"You two fighting about something?"

"No." Chase stalked over to Dani, placed his hand behind her head and gave her a hard kiss. To show Trent and her and himself that she belonged to him—would belong to him for ever—no matter what the obstacles. No matter how stubborn she was.

Her shocked eyes widened and she opened her mouth to speak but Chase had had enough talking for one morning. He dropped his hand. "I'm going to check on Drew before I take a shower." He knew his voice was tight, barely controlled, but it was better than yelling at both of them, which was what he wanted to do. "See you in the clinic."

"See, that wasn't so bad, was it?" Dani rubbed the arm of the little girl she'd just immunized and smiled, holding out a sheet of the stickers she'd brought from the States for the girl to choose from. The child's dark eyes lit up at a sparkly fairy, and she carefully stuck it to the big index card Dani gave her.

With any luck, the children's families would pay attention and bring both the child and the card back when her next shots were due. Of course, they didn't have calendars so they would doubtless have trouble remembering exactly when they should return. And, sadly, most couldn't even read. But the double system, with Dani having the information entered into the laptop, too, just might help keep track of their care better than before. If and when they showed up again.

Spud and the local nurses had gone into different communities to let people know they'd be doing immunizations all week, and it seemed to have worked pretty well. Trent had the day off, but she and Chase managed the substantial turnout.

Dani was surprised and thrilled with the slow but steady stream of children that arrived, some on bicycles, some on scooters, some on foot. One entire family showed up in a rickety horse-drawn cart, and Chase had teased her again about not being in Kansas any more, as it was apparently a common occurrence.

Dani smiled at the next child in line and, for at least the fiftieth time that day, found herself momentarily distracted by Chase standing ten feet across the room. Her gaze catching on his profile as he listened with his stethoscope. Staring at the strong muscles in his arms, his big gentle hands as they moved over a patient's body. The creases in the corners of his eyes as he caught her looking and gave her a knowing smile that showed he, too, was remembering last night.

This was exactly why she'd practically run from the room. Chase was a dangerous drug she wasn't sure she should keep taking. Bringing a euphoria that made her want to forget about anything but the scent of his skin, the delicious feel of his heavy body atop hers, the mind-blowing pleasure only he had ever given her.

She just might have been able to resist his magnetic pull. Stayed strong despite the way her pulse tripped and her breathing suspended every time he touched or teased her. But watching his amazing work yesterday had filled her with awe. Not that she'd forgotten what he did every day. What miracles he could accomplish when a situation demanded it.

But seeing how disturbed he'd obviously felt after the difficult birth of the baby and nearly losing the mother, combined with the admiration that had filled her heart, had touched the healer in her.

It seemed obvious he must have been thinking about Drew and how blessed they both were that their son had been born without complications. Asking to see pictures of Drew as a baby and toddler must mean he'd been painfully thinking about having missed those years.

She hadn't made a conscious decision to give in to her desire to be with him. But when she'd seen the haunted look in his eyes, she'd wanted to make it all better. To bring back the normally tough and confident Dr. Chase Bowen who never showed the vulnerability that had so surprised her.

Even now there was tenseness about his mouth and eyes. Edginess that had been there when he'd given her that hard kiss in the kitchen right in front of Trent. Like he had been staking his claim.

She dragged her attention back to the child she was about to immunize. The bad news was that their lovemaking had done more than momentarily take the strain from Chase's face. It had touched the wound deep in her heart she'd thought had healed and scarred over. The wound she absolutely did not want ripped open again.

But apparently her self-protective mechanism wasn't working quite right, because she couldn't stop thinking about what they'd shared last night. Couldn't stop thinking about how wonderful and special and overwhelming it had been, and how she wanted it again.

Which was very, very dangerous.

You'd think she'd never made love to him before. Hadn't spent an entire year exploring every inch of Chase's body in every possible location.

Disgusted with herself for thinking about every inch of his body for the hundredth time that day, Dani finished the little girl's immunizations. She looked around the room and saw Chase locking some drugs in the drawer.

He must have felt her gaze on him because his brown eyes met hers. "Need some help?" Chase asked.

She turned back to her work table, smiling at a little boy now ready for his shots. "A back rub would be nice. I feel like my spine is frozen in a permanently bent position."

And wasn't that kind of invitation a totally stupid thing to say? She gulped and focused on making the boy feel at ease as she poked him with a needle. Suddenly, right next to her, Chase placed his hands on her shoulders, gently kneading, lowering his head next to hers. "I'm very good at the kind of doctoring where we find a new position for your back. I can make it feel all better."

The sensual promise in his voice took her right back to last night, suspending her breath and making her heart flutter. The boy she'd just immunized left with his stickered card clutched to his chest and she glanced up at Chase. At the curve of his lips. At his eyes, smoldering and dark. And somehow shadowed, too, with something else she couldn't figure out. Worry? She'd thought that was her domain.

"How's that feel? Better?"

"Yes. Good. Thanks, that's enough." She stood and stepped to a cupboard, gulping in oxygen not infused with Chase's scent.

Why, oh, why did her body and mind so want to get physical with him again, instead of listening to logic? But it was more than obvious it would take very little persuasion on his part to start what they'd had last night all over again.

And why not? that traitorous part of her brain whispered. Just like last night, she was finding it harder and harder to come up with a good reason why she couldn't just enjoy the unbelievable way he made her feel. To give herself up to it until he left.

Until he left. How she'd feel then, she had no clue. Tough as it had been leaving him three years ago, she'd survived it. Even managed to stop thinking about him constantly. Stopped wondering where he was and what he was doing and who he was doing it with.

But this time would be different, and that knowledge brought heaviness to her chest and a painful stab to her soul.

This time, because they had Drew to share, she'd be in contact with him. Know all that she hadn't known before, including if he had a serious relationship with someone else. That most definitely would not be a good feeling, but she'd have to toughen up and deal with it. The question was, would making love with him or not making love with him while they were here together make it any less painful in the future?

Was it worth the risk to her heart to fall headlong into the heady, emotional crevasse that was Chase Bowen? A crevasse she'd foolishly thought three years ago that he'd fallen into along with her?

Through the doorway the sun glowed low in the sky and the tall man walking in seemed to bring a sweep of muggy heat along with him. He wore a cylinder-shaped striped hat and a bright and colorful tunic completely at odds with the grim exhaustion etched on his face. A boy of about fourteen followed him. Nearly expressionless except for his deeply somber eyes, he had a length of equally bright fabric wrapped around his shoulders and arms like a cape.

Chase stepped over to them and spoke to the man, who turned to the boy with a single nod. Like an unveiling, the child slipped the fabric from his arms.

Dani's breath stopped and she stared in disbelief. She'd thought Apollo had had a terrible injury? This was something straight out of a horror movie.

CHAPTER ELEVEN

TWO LONG BARE bones stuck out below the child's elbow from what was left of his arm. The normal soft tissue abruptly ended, with the skin black and mummified.

Dani could hardly believe what she was seeing. Her chest constricted at what unimaginable pain the boy had to have suffered over what must have been weeks, or even longer. Clearly his hand had completely rotted off and left behind what they were staring at.

Dani lifted her gaze to Chase's. His expression was carefully neutral as he asked questions of the father and the boy. But his dark eyes held grave despair.

"Okay." Chase's chest rose and fell in a deep breath as he turned those eyes to Dani. "I don't have to tell you we have to remove what's left of his arm. I'll take it off above the elbow. You'll have to act as my assistant. If you don't want to, we can have them spend the night and I'll have Trent or the nurse help me tomorrow."

"Of course I'll assist." Did he think she couldn't handle the tough stuff? She'd feel insulted if the situation wasn't so awful.

"Let's get him set up in the OR. I'll scrub then get him anesthetized."

With a few quick words to the father he laid his hand gently on the boy's back and guided him through the doors to the OR. Dani tried to give a reassuring smile to the man, reaching out to touch his forearm, trying to let him know it would be okay, but the man's expression didn't change.

The ache in her chest intensified, imagining what not only the boy but his parents, too, had been through with this. Why, oh, why hadn't they come in sooner? It was a miracle that infection hadn't killed the child.

As she entered the room, she was struck by the stoic expression on the boy's face. Just lying there, quiet and still, looking at her and Chase with serious, deep brown eyes. Not upset. Not even grim. Just accepting of this horrible thing that had happened to him, which would affect him for the rest of his life. She swallowed down tears and busied herself getting the surgical equipment together.

Chase put the boy under sedation with some antiquated-looking equipment. "I've never seen a machine like this," Dani said, both because she wondered about it and to distract her from what was about to happen. "Does it ever fail?"

"It looks like hell, I know. But it's reliable and safe, believe it or not. A hospital in Cotonou donated it."

Dani watched Chase prep the skin above the boy's elbow, waiting for him to tell her the story about the child. When he said nothing, she had to ask. "Did they tell you what happened? Why they waited so long to come in?"

"This kind of thing happens way too often." Chase picked up the knife. "He fell from a tree. They live over sixty kilometers away, with no easy way to get here."

Dani thought about Drew learning to shinny up the palm tree, at the climbing competitions Evelyn and Phil had told her about, and her heart stopped. "If kids fall from trees all the time, why do parents allow it? Why did *you* do it?"

"They're not climbing for fun. They're gathering leaves for their livestock. During the drought that can follow the rainy season, there isn't enough food to feed the animals. After a long time working in the trees, they get careless or just lose their footing."

Chase seemed fiercely focused on making a circumferential, fish-mouth incision above the child's elbow to leave plenty of skin and flesh to fold beneath what would end up being the stump of his arm. Dani noted the tightness of his lips, his jaws clamped together, and knew that, no matter how many times he'd seen these kinds of horrific things, he never got used to it. Never just took it in his stride but felt deep empathy for all the people born without the privileges so many others took for granted.

She suddenly saw what she hadn't completely understood before. Why he'd said this wasn't just what he did but who he was.

He had been born into this life. Accomplished

more in a year to help people on this earth than most did in a lifetime. And she again felt overwhelmed with the admiration and respect she'd felt yesterday. Had felt in Honduras when she'd seen the lives he'd changed.

From the moment she'd met him, she knew he was like no one she'd met before. And with painful clarity, she understood even more what a nearly insurmountable situation yawned between them. His work was his life, and while he wanted to be a good father, he'd never be able to be that unless they lived together. He didn't want Drew anywhere but the U.S., but she, too, wanted to make at least a small contribution to people like this young boy. So where did that leave them?

There was no good answer. Marriage? Leaving her alone and Drew wondering why his dad didn't want to live with them? No marriage? Leaving them even more distant from one another? Dear Lord, she just didn't know.

Chase clamped off the artery and vein then reached for the bone saw. As he sawed through the humerus she clenched her teeth at the horrific sound and thought of her own son. Wanted to know more about why the family had waited until the situation was this bad.

"Why didn't they come in sooner?"

"I told you. They live far away. Just spent two days walking here. Obviously, it was a compound fracture, and the local healer tried splinting it and called on the spirit Sakpata to help him heal. They probably thought it would be okay. But I'm sure it was full of debris just like Apollo's and got infected."

He set aside the bone that would never again be a part of the child. With heavy sadness weighing in her chest, she pressed sponges against the opening to soak up blood and fluids. "But they must have seen that it wasn't getting better. I can't even imagine what it must have looked like."

"Don't judge them. Don't impose your Western views on the life they have to live here." His voice was fierce as he clamped off the artery and vein and began to sew the fish-mouth incision back together over the stump. "They didn't know what to think. Thought maybe it was healing, part of Sakpata's plan when his hand turned from pink to purple to black."

He leaned more closely over the gaping, raw flesh, carefully stitching the tissue. "But, as you can tell, there was superficial dry gangrene of the exposed tissue. He must have a good immune system, which sealed the gangrene off in the junction between the wound and the rest of his arm. Kept him alive. By the time his hand was mummified and hanging on by just the neurofiber bundle, they knew it was too late."

"My God," she whispered, and tears stung her eyes again. It was hard to even process what the child had gone through.

Chase glanced at her, and his grim expression softened slightly. "Please don't cry. It doesn't accomplish a damned thing. These people are tough and used to challenges we can't even imagine. To absolute hell being handed to them on a platter."

A tear spilled over and Dani lifted her shoulder to swipe it away. "I'm not as hardened as you are to all this."

"I hope I'm not hardened." He laughed without any humor in the sound at all. "I'm just determined. Determined to get more doctors and nurses in places like this. Determined to get more

funding. And as much as you might not understand his parents letting this happen, I give the
father huge credit for bringing him in now. I've
seen people who lived with something this bad
for years that was never addressed by modern
medicine."

She looked at him, at the intensity in his eyes
as he worked. "If more doctors are needed here,
why are you so determined that I take Drew to
live in the States? Why wouldn't you just want
us to stay here? For me to work alongside you?"
Wasn't that the obvious solution? He claimed to
want her to marry him. At least that way they'd
be together as a family.

"Didn't you just hear me say it can be hell in
a place like this? Drew doesn't belong here. Not
until he's an adult."

"It's not the same thing for him as it is for the
people who live here. Obviously, he wouldn't be
exposed to the same problems."

"To some of them he would." His anger seemed
to ratchet higher, practically radiating from him
as he pinned her with a ferocious gaze. "He can-
not and will not live in developing countries. Pe-

riod. Now, are you going to just stand there or are you going to help?"

Sheesh. "Yes, Dr. Bowen." She couldn't remember him ever being this domineering and cranky before. Must be the stress of this poor boy's injury compounded by the stress of their personal situation.

She grabbed thin suture material and handed it to Chase to finish tying off the artery and vein, then continued to sponge out the blood as he worked. There was clearly no talking to the man once his mind was made up, and now wasn't the right time anyway. Though, so far, there hadn't seemed to be any right time to come up with a solution they could agree on.

"While I finish the ligation of the artery and the stitching, you can pull together the sterile cotton dressing and elastic wrap."

When it was over, all that was left of the child's arm was a stump neatly rounded in a compression dressing. Dani wondered if he'd be relieved at no longer looking at his own bones, or if the final loss of his arm would grieve him, too.

Her heart squeezed. As Chase had said, the

boy had been handed hell and, unlike in the U.S., would probably never have a prosthesis that would give him a usable limb. Her own mom had always told her to remember that life wasn't fair, and wasn't that the truth? Next time she felt like complaining about something, she'd step back and picture this boy's arm and his tragically stoic expression.

They settled the boy into a bed, and Chase told the father they could stay for three days until it was time to change the dressing.

"Usually, we'd just send him home tomorrow and have them come back to have the dressing changed in a few days, as we're pretty full up in the hospital," Chase said as they headed out the doors to find Drew. "But I bet they wouldn't come back, because they live so far away. We can't risk infection."

Dani nodded, and they continued walking, not saying anything. His expression was still grim and she wasn't sure if it was because of the boy or their conversation about Drew or both. She felt emotionally spent from the whole experience and, really, what more was there to say?

"I forgot to tell you," Chase said, shoving his hands in his pockets as they walked side by side. "Mom has a bee in her bonnet about going to some hotel in Parakou that a friend of theirs owns before they leave. It's about thirty kilometers from here. Wants to have lunch there. I guess there's a nice pool too, and as we have tomorrow off, she wants us to take Drew swimming. Is that okay with you?"

"Drew doesn't know how to swim. He's only two." Climbing trees and swimming with the child barely out of diapers? What was with this family?

"Two and a half," he said, his expression lightening in a slight smile. "I'll teach him. The sooner he learns, the better."

"I assume you won't just throw him in the deep end and tell him to flap his arms and kick?"

"Don't worry. I'll show him the basic moves before I send him off the diving board."

"Chase!" She stared at him then frowned as he chuckled. He'd always delighted in teasing her, and too often she fell for it.

He put his arm around her shoulders. "I promise not to scare him. We'll just have fun. He won't learn how to be really safe in the water for a while, but it's a first step."

Apparently his anger with her had cooled, as he touched his warm lips to her temple, lingering there for a moment, sending a tingle across her cheek and down her neck. "If it works out, we could probably take him to the hotel weekly, even though Mom and Dad will be gone."

She looked into his deep brown eyes and wanted to ask the question hanging between them. What was going to happen when he was gone, too?

"Sure. Sounds fun. I'd like to see more of the countryside. And another city."

"Good." He stopped walking, and since his arm was around her she stopped, too. He used his free hand to cup her cheek and gave her a soft kiss she should have stepped away from. Should have prevented from quickly morphing into something hotter, needier.

His tongue slipped inside her mouth and the taste of him was so delicious, so overwhelming she couldn't resist. One tiny taste. One more minute. One more time.

On their own, her arms wrapped around his waist and held tight as he moved his hands down her body, firm and sure and insistent. One large palm cupped her behind as his other hand slipped beneath her shirt, caressing her skin, making her gasp as he pulled her close against his hardened body.

His lips separated a whisper from hers, his breath quick against her moist skin. "Dani." His mouth covered hers again, slanted to deepen it, intensify the taste and feel of his kiss, and the heat between them became so scorching she was sure she just might combust right there outside the building.

He tore his mouth from hers, his eyes passion-glazed and nearly black as he stared at her. "How about that back rub? Like now, and naked?"

Now and naked sounded very, very good, but the moment without his lips on hers gave her enough time to gather a tiny semblance of sanity. A second to protect her heart. "I just…don't know if that's a good idea. I admit last night was wonderful. But I'm afraid it just makes things more…confusing."

She pulled out of his arms completely, regretting no longer having his arms around her, his fingers touching her skin, his mouth igniting hers. But her brain told her she should stay strong. Wouldn't having sex, being together again intimately, just lead to heartache?

For a moment he didn't speak, and she wasn't sure what emotions flickered across his face. Frustration? Contemplation? Agreement? She was surprised he didn't reach for her again, and quickly turned to continue into the building before something else happened that might put her yet again under his spell. Again weaken her resolve.

"Dani—"

"Let's not talk about any of this right now." She kept going, counting the steps to the door. Maybe it was cowardly, but she needed a minute to regroup. Some time to get her breath back and her heart back into a normal rhythm. Some time to figure out the confusing messages her brain and body kept sending through every nerve. "After your parents leave, we'll sit down together and discuss options. When we make some decisions, I promise to be reasonable."

He grasped her arm and stopped her progress, turning her to him. His gaze no longer passionate or angry, he looked beyond serious. "Reasonable is marrying the man who cares about you and our son. Reasonable is planning our future together. I don't get what's not obvious about that."

"Because I don't want to be married to someone who doesn't live with me. I don't want Drew to wonder why his father's work is more important to him than he is." *I don't want to be hurt again.* "Why don't you understand that?"

"Dani." He cupped her face in his hands, and the tender and sincere expression on his face gripped her heart. "I promise I'll be with you as much as I can. I've already talked with the GPC and asked about eight-month assignments. I admit it'll be hard for me to adjust to working in the States some, but I'm willing to do it. For Drew and for you. What more can I say and do to convince you it will work out?"

Maybe the words *I love you*? She wanted to say

it aloud—nearly did—but bit the inside of her cheek just in time. She'd refused to even think about that being part of the equation. Until last night. Until they'd practically set the bed on fire and her along with it. Their time together brought back every single memory of the intense physical and emotional intimacy they'd shared in Honduras.

True, he had told her he loved her back in Honduras. Once or twice had uttered those three little, wonderful-to-hear words.

Then he'd turned her down flat when she'd asked him to marry her, saying he just wasn't the marrying kind. Knowing that he only wanted to marry her now because of Drew still pained her more than she wanted to admit.

Was she able to be in the kind of marriage he was offering? Would it be okay for Drew? Could she convince Chase how important it was to her to spend at least some time doing mission work? After a few years, would Chase feel a need to work full time outside the U.S. again, leaving them alone almost all year?

She didn't know. And all the uncertainty

weighed heavily in her chest. All the questions spun in circles in her mind.

"Like I said last night, I need time to think." She tried hard to ignore the delicious feel of his thumb gently sliding across her cheekbone, his breath touching her skin. "I've asked you before, and I'm asking again. Please stop pushing for an answer. Let's let…things unfold…as they will. Without you confusing me with your hot kisses."

"Since you think my kisses are hot," he said, a smile finally touching his lips, "and you asked nicely, I'll be good. For how long I can't say, but I'll try."

He touched his mouth to hers, light and quick, and the, oh, so brief touch still made her feel weak. His five o'clock shadow gently abraded her cheek as he whispered in her ear, "If you change your mind tonight, though, you know where my bed is."

CHAPTER TWELVE

"EAT UP YOUR breakfast so we can get going," Dani told Drew as he fidgeted on the kitchen stool, just poking at his oatmeal. "I've already got your swimsuit and everything packed. We're waiting for you."

"I ready to go."

"Not until you eat." Her cellphone rang and she pulled it from her pocket, wondering who could be calling.

"Dr. Sheridan here." She touched Drew's hand, mimed him eating, then jabbed her finger at his bowl.

"Hello, Dr. Sheridan, this is Colleen Mason from GPC. How are you?"

"Fine. How can I help you?" She picked up Drew's spoon and poked oatmeal in his mouth, to his frowning annoyance.

"I'm Director Mike Hardy's assistant. I wanted

to let you know that your request for a transfer to Panama has been granted, and we have arranged for a replacement for you in Benin. You'll start four weeks from today. Would you like for me to make all your travel arrangements?"

"I'm sorry, there must be some mistake. I didn't ask for a transfer to Panama."

"This is Dr. Danielle Sheridan? Currently in Benin?"

"Yes." What a weird error. "But I'm scheduled to stay here for eight months, and I only arrived a week ago."

"Well, I'm confused now. I'll have to check with Mike, but it was my understanding that you're scheduled to relocate with Dr. Bowen at the same time he goes to work in Panama."

Her breath backed up in her lungs and she nearly dropped her phone. "Dr. Chase Bowen? Is he moving to Panama?"

"Yes. The same date I have you scheduled to go."

Shock and anger welled up in her chest and threatened to choke her. It didn't take a genius to realize this was no mistake. That this was the work of a certain master manipulator determined to have everything his way and make decisions for her, and to heck with talking to her about it beforehand.

She could barely catch her breath to speak. "Well, I'm afraid this is a mistake. I have no intention of moving to Panama. Let me speak with Dr. Bowen and I'll call you back."

"All right. And I'll speak with Mike, too, to see what the mix-up is. Thanks."

Normally, Dani was pretty easygoing and couldn't remember ever feeling quite like this. Her whole body shook and her head tingled with fury. "Eat your food, Drew. I'll be right back."

She stalked towards the door but before she could push it open to go find the controlling man and let him have it, the jerk in question walked in.

"The car's packed up. Are you—?"

She flattened both hands against his chest and gave him a shove. "Who do you think you are?"

His eyes widened and his brows rose practically to his hairline. "What?"

Her jaw clenched, she glanced back at Drew to see him finally eating, and grabbed Chase's arm.

She pulled him into the hall and had to rein in her desire to pummel him with her fists just to release the wild anger welling within her.

"You're moving to Panama." She dragged in a breath so she could speak past the pounding of her heart. "You didn't even tell me. And you didn't even ask what I thought about moving there and working there with you. You just decided Drew and I should go and that's that?"

The surprise on his face settled into grim seriousness. "Okay. I get it that you're upset. Let me explain."

"There's no explanation necessary. It's pretty obvious what you think."

Her anger morphed into a different emotion, and she found herself swallowing a huge lump in her throat and the tears that threatened to accompany it.

Now she knew. Knew how she'd feel when he moved away. And it was so much worse, so much more painful than she'd expected. As she stared at his face, she knew without a doubt she'd miss him horribly. Even more than when she'd left Honduras, though she would never have dreamed that was possible.

And Drew. Drew would miss the daddy he'd so easily embraced and now loved to be with. What she'd feared and dreaded all along.

But moving with him? What would that solve?

Nothing. It would just delay the inevitable. She and Drew would move back to the States when her contract was up, but Chase wouldn't. It was as simple and wretched as that.

"I'm not moving to Panama with you. I'm not moving anywhere with you."

He grasped her arms and narrowed his eyes, his voice tight. "Listen. Panama is safer for Drew than Africa. And it would give us almost eight more months together, for you to think about us. For you to see we belong together. I'm not leaving here without this resolved between us."

"Then don't leave." She tipped her chin and stared at him. The man she knew never backed down from a challenge. "Stay here. Tell the GPC you're taking a leave of absence."

"I can't do that." Now he too was angry, his brows deeply furrowed over fierce brown eyes. "I have a contract with them. I have work to do."

"Well, so do I." She tried to shake free of his grip, but he held her tight. "This is why—"

"Is our baby ready to go?"

Evelyn's cheerful voice came down the hall with her and Phil, but both of them stopped short near the kitchen door.

"I'm sorry." Chase's parents looked at them with obvious uneasiness. "Are we…still on for today? Would you like us to take Drew by ourselves?"

"No. We're coming." Chase released Dani's arms and his chest rose and fell as his expression cooled into stone. "Where's Drew?"

"Eating. I'm sure he's done."

Without another word she stepped into the kitchen to gather up her son and his gear. Drew deserved a nice day with his grandparents, who were leaving tomorrow, and his daddy, who was leaving very soon. Before they went back to life as it had been. Back to just the two of them.

So much for worrying about Drew maybe being intimidated by the swimming pool. Dani sat with Evelyn at an ornate wrought iron table and watched her son splash with delight in the warm, crystal-clear water.

Drew's silliness and his grandparents' laughter at everything he did and said had made the drive to the hotel bearable. Had given Dani time to cool off, toughen up, and accept that Chase was leaving. To swallow that pain. To even forgive his audacity at trying to get them moved with him, because he thought, in his twisted sort of way, that it would have given them more time together. How could she really be angry about that?

No, her anger had proved to be as fleeting as their relationship had been. And she was left with only bleak resignation weighing heavily on the depths of her soul.

Chase stood in the shallow end of the pool, holding their son's little body with both hands around his ribs while Phil tossed him a plastic ball, and she had to admit the child looked practically ready to do breaststroke.

Breaststroke. An unfortunate name for a swimming position that made her think, with an ache in her heart, about their time together last night. Since he was leaving, she figured she deserved to stare at Chase's half-naked body. To imprint it one last time upon her memory.

She'd had her turn in the pool with Drew before they'd taken a break for lunch. Twists of both pain and pleasure had knotted her stomach as Chase had watched her swim with Drew. With his eyelids low, his gaze had been filled with the same emotions swirling through her now. A heightened sensual awareness tempered by frustration and dejection.

After having chlorine repeatedly stinging her eyes, she'd been more than happy to hand Drew over to Chase, quickly moving across the tiled floor because having her damp body brushing against his skin was torture. Thankfully, the hotel gift shop had a white terrycloth swimsuit cover-up she could buy, as she wasn't about to sit there in a bikini in front of Chase. Or while sitting next to his mother.

At first she'd tried hard not to eye Chase in the pool the way he'd eyed her, but failed miserably. The wetness of his bronzed skin seemed to emphasize every inch of his muscled strength. As he dunked Drew partway into the water then back up, to the child's laughing delight, his biceps bulged and his six-pack rippled, and the dark, wet hair in the center of his chest ran in a damp arrow to disappear beneath his black swim trunks. Why couldn't the man be growing a paunch and losing his hair?

"Our Andrew is a fish, just like his father," Evelyn said.

Dani yanked her attention back to Chase's mother, thankful Evelyn was watching the action in the pool instead of noticing the way she was staring at the woman's son. Evelyn wore what seemed like a permanent expression of happy pride, and Dani felt gratified and blessed that Chase's parents already adored their grandchild.

"Is Chase a fish?" She tried to remember if she'd ever seen him actually swim, but could only come up with the times the two of them had splashed in waterfalls with shallow pools. Not that she'd be surprised, since he seemed to be good at everything physical. Which started her thoughts down that painful path again, and that had to stop. Chase wouldn't be around to show her his various physical skills, and she again pulled her attention back to Evelyn.

"Oh, yes. Many of the places we lived had

lakes. When he was older, he started doing tri-athlons and trained in the ocean when we lived somewhere near a coast." She smiled, obviously enjoying the memories. "When we worked at big hospitals, he was on a few swim teams and won a number of trophies. He and Brady would swim laps for ever, it seemed, though, of course, Chase lasted longest as he was older."

Brady. Obviously, Chase's brother. "I hope you don't mind if I ask you about Brady," she said quietly. "Chase has never talked about him."

"No, he wouldn't." She sighed, her eyes shad-owed as she stared at the pool. "It was a terrible thing for all of us when Brady died."

Dani sat without speaking, hoping she'd con-tinue. Eventually, though, she had to ask her to elaborate. "What happened?" she asked gently.

"We were living in the Congo. Working at a small hospital there. Chase was sixteen, Brady fourteen." Evelyn turned her now serious gaze to Dani. "We knew it must be malaria, though, of course, we'd taken the usual precautions. Took one chloroquine once a week. Had mosquito net-ting over the beds and used repellent."

Her expression grew grimmer as she turned her gaze to the pool again. "But Brady presented with high fever. Was lethargic. We immediately gave him more chloroquine and kept an eye on him, giving him fluids." She closed her eyes for a moment. "But he got sicker. We tried quinine with the chloroquine but after another couple days, he couldn't eat or drink. We put a tube down his nose to rehydrate him, but knew we had to get him home to a U.S. hospital."

"Did Chase go with you?" Dani could only imagine how scared a sixteen-year-old boy would be when his beloved brother was so sick. Or maybe, as a teenager, he hadn't fully understood how serious it was.

Evelyn shook her head. "No. And that was a mistake. He was in the middle of mid-term exams, had his friends there, and we were blindly sure that, once in the States, Brady would get better." She turned her brown gaze on Dani, and tears filled her eyes. "But he didn't. Turned out he had a strain of malaria resistant to chloroquine. The malaria went into his brain and it was over."

"I'm so sorry." Dani's throat closed, and she rested her hand on the older woman's arm, knowing the touch was little comfort. What else was there to say? An unimaginable loss for any parent.

Evelyn nodded and wiped away her tears. "It was a terrible time for all of us. But in some ways it was worst for Chase. He never got to say goodbye to Brady. Wasn't there at the end, holding his hand, like we were. It wasn't his fault, but I know he felt guilty and selfish that he'd stayed in Africa to take a test and hang with his friends instead of being there for his brother."

Finally, Dani saw everything very clearly, as though she'd been looking through binoculars and had suddenly found how to focus them.

She saw why Chase was so insistent that Drew not live in Africa. Or any developing country. He'd experienced first hand the worst that could happen.

Obviously, it was also why he hadn't wanted children, ever. Doctoring the neediest of humankind, as he'd so often said, was what he did. Who he was. And he couldn't do that, and be that, with a family he wanted to keep safe.

His rejection of her marriage proposal hadn't been all about him, as she'd long assumed. About having a woman in every port, so to speak, which she'd bitterly wondered after she'd left. It was about his deep caring for others, and she should have known that all along.

"Thank you for telling me, Evelyn," Dani said. "I would guess you're in agreement with Chase that I shouldn't have Drew here in Africa."

Evelyn gave her a sad smile. "There are risks no matter where you live. I'm not sure what the right answers are. I do know Chase didn't particularly like living in the States."

But he wanted her and Drew there. "Do you know why not?"

"We sent him to a boarding school for a year after Brady died, and he hated it. He was too used to living in unusual places around the world with all different kinds of people and couldn't tolerate what he saw as the superficial things important to American kids of his own age." A genuine smile lit her face, banishing the shadows. "I told him he's a reverse snob. That it's okay to want to have nice things and live in a nice house. It's all a matter of balance."

Wasn't that true about life in general? Balance. It was what she needed to find with Chase in their decisions about Drew. Marriage or no marriage.

"Don't look so stressed, dear." It was Evelyn's turn to press a reassuring hand to Dani's forearm. "I know my son can be a bit on the domineering side when he makes up his mind, but things will work out the way they're meant to. I don't know why you kept Andrew a secret from Chase, but after meeting you I would guess you had your reasons. Now that we have Andrew in our lives, you already know we're here to stay."

"Yes." Dani looked at the steadiness in Evelyn's eyes, the warmth, and knew Chase had been blessed with special parents as he'd grown up. Part of what had shaped him to be the special man he was today. "I do know."

CHAPTER THIRTEEN

BY THE TIME they returned from Parakou, the moon was rising and darkness was closing in. Spud had a simple, late meal waiting for them, ready to be warmed.

Swimming was clearly an exhausting activity, as Drew's eyes kept closing at dinner, his face nearly dropping into his plate of spaghetti. With his grandparents chuckling, Dani decided there was no hope in trying to get more food in the child that night. She followed Chase as he carried Drew, barely able to awaken him enough to get bedtime necessities done before he was in a deep sleep.

Dani pulled Drew's covers over his shoulders and kissed his cheek, his little rosebud lips already parted in deep slumber. "'Night, baby boy."

She pulled the mosquito netting around the bed before turning to Chase in the darkened room. He stood there with his hands in his pockets, staring at her with such intense concentration it was almost unnerving.

"I guess we should get back to dinner," she said. "Help clean up."

He stood silently for another long moment before he finally spoke. "Thank you for today. I know my parents had a great time with you and Drew. And I did, too."

"I couldn't believe how much he loved the water. You were right—at this rate he's going to be swimming before his next birthday."

He placed his wide palm against his chest and raised his eyebrows. "Did I hear you say I was right about something? I need to sit down."

"I'm pretty sure I give you credit when you actually *are* right. Which does happen occasionally," she said, trying to lighten the mood, which had weighed heavily on both of them all afternoon.

He didn't even smile, his serious eyes seeming to study her. Maybe he could see what she was thinking. Feeling. Finally understanding.

"I'm…sorry about the Panama thing. It was

wrong of me to not talk to you. I just…" He shoved his hand into his hair. "I felt desperate. I don't want to leave without you agreeing we should get married. Without us *being* married."

After learning what she had today about his brother, she understood much more than she had just hours earlier. And the pain of his rejection when she had proposed to him didn't hurt quite as much as it had before.

As she looked into his eyes, she allowed herself to see what she hadn't looked for back then. Hadn't bothered to observe. The vulnerability deep within their chocolaty depths when all she'd noticed had been his utter confidence. His utter determination.

What must it have been like for him to be living his carefree teenage life, focused on school and his friends, only to lose his brother so suddenly and shockingly? The fact that she'd known Chase for over a year and he'd never mentioned it showed her he still carried the pain of it deep inside.

"I'm not ready to make a commitment to marriage, Chase. But I understand things better now."

She clasped his hand. "We have a little time before you go to Panama. When you leave…"

He pressed his finger to her lips. "Shh. I don't want to talk. I don't even want you to say you'll marry me right now. We've done too much talking in circles, arguing, trying to figure out what to do and how to do it. All I want is to kiss you and be with you." He cupped her face in his hands and gave her the softest of kisses, and like before, it was too much and not nearly enough.

Too much to be able to walk away, feeling nothing. Not nearly enough to satisfy the craving her body couldn't help but feel for him. The craving she was no longer trying to resist.

She wanted those same soft kisses everywhere on her body.

Need bloomed within her as she wrapped her arms around his body and pulled him close, her breasts tingling at the heavy beat of his heart against them. "The only talking I was going to do was to say, 'Make love to me.'"

His lips curved and his eyes gleamed in the low light. "Now, that kind of talking I'm good with."

He kissed her, soft, teasing, coaxing. But coaxing wasn't necessary. The moment his mouth covered hers, gently drawing her tongue inside to dance slowly with his, she was lost. He tipped his head to one side, exploring her mouth so thoroughly she could barely breathe. His fingers pressed into her hips and pulled her against his hard body. Her heart thumped hard against her ribs and just as she sank deeply into his kiss, fumbling at the button of his shorts, wanting him so much her knees wobbled, his hands dropped to her shoulders and he set her away from him.

She stared at him, confused. His eyes smoldered, dark and dangerous, and the curve of his lips promised all things carnal and wonderful. So why wasn't he touching her? "What—?"

"I found a place for us that's a little more fun than a bed." His voice was low and sexy. "More like what we enjoyed in Honduras. For days, I've been thinking about you and me, there, naked under the stars. Let's get in the car and go."

She couldn't wait to make love with him, and he wanted to go on a road trip? "We made love in a bed plenty of times in Honduras. I'm for that. Your room. Like now."

He laughed, a deep, smoky rumble. "I like it when you're all bossy." He pulled her close again for a hard, intense kiss that was over all too soon before he set her away from him and pulled his phone from his pocket.

She folded her arms across her thumping heart, staring at his phone in disbelief. "You going to call 911 for help? Good idea, because I just might have to hurt you if you don't immediately demonstrate some of your amazing sexual skills."

That low laugh of his, louder this time, seemed to reverberate in her own chest. He pressed his palm to her mouth. "We agreed on no talking, remember?" With that annoying smile still on his face, he lowered his head to nibble her neck, her lobe, his moist tongue touching the shell of her ear. "Unless the subject is sex. So let me tell you what I want to do to you."

His breath slipped across her skin and the rumble of his voice was filled with desire. "First, I want…"

"Less talk, more action." She slipped her hands inside his T-shirt, up the smooth skin of his ribs to lightly abrade his nipples with her short fingernails as she ran her mouth across his jaw. Beneath her hands, his heart pounded and his muscles bunched.

"To strip off all your clothes and see every inch of your skin," he continued in that deep voice so full of sexual promise she about threw him down on her bed to get on with it. "All day you teased me, wearing that little bitty swimsuit of yours. I want to—"

"Get naked and horizontal right this second?" She slipped her hand down into his shorts, seeking the biggest object of her desire.

He quickly pulled her hand out of his pants and heaved a breath. "You always were an impatient cheat." He texted into his phone as she massaged the hard ridge beneath his zipper. He grabbed her wrist again with a breathless laugh. "Damn it, stop."

"You kiss me until I can't remember my name then say stop?" Nearly dizzy with wanting him, she forced herself to step to the bed and sat, but the distance barely slowed the aching heat pooling low in her body. "Fine."

If he planned on continuing his hard-to-get

game, he was in for a surprise. On alert, she watched him, ready to make her move. Which would be that as soon as he came close enough, she'd pounce and yank him down next to her.

Yeah. She felt her own lips curve, anticipating what fun it was going to be, wrestling around on the bed and stripping off their clothes. Somehow she doubted he'd keep up the delay tactics and resist.

Except he was still looking at his phone, and her amusement faded into downright irritation. All the teasing all week, even their lovemaking of a few nights ago, had left him cool and in control while she was practically melting for him?

Then the surprise move was his. Two steps to the bed, and he effortlessly scooped her up into his arms. With quick strides he carried her out into the hall.

Okay, maybe he had a good plan after all. She pressed closer, wrapping her arms around his neck and nibbling at his lips. Beneath her hands, his back muscles flexed and tightened. "I hate to remind you," she said, giving his lips a teasing lick that left his own tongue chasing after hers, "but we can't just leave Drew."

"What, you thought I was texting my broker?" He practically kicked open the door and carried her out into the warm, sultry night. "Mom says she'll watch Drew."

Her blood began to pump faster and her body hummed in anticipation. He'd thought to call for babysitting, which must mean he had something very delicious in mind. She ran her mouth across his skin, loving the taste of him, the curve of his jaw, the slight abrasion of his skin.

"If you don't stop, we're not going to make it any farther than the backseat of this car." His eyes glinted down at her, eyelids half-closed, and it wasn't too dark to see that the smile was gone from his face, replaced by a hunger that was exactly what she wanted to see. The same hunger rising within her and leaving her breathless.

He yanked open the door of the Land Rover and practically dumped her inside, before shutting the door and jogging to the driver's side.

The engine grumbled to life and Chase hit the

gas, apparently in a hurry. And that was fine with Dani.

Wondering why such an old car had bucket seats instead of a nice, long bench, she attempted to cuddle up close to him, touching her lips to his chin, his cheek, his ear. It wasn't too difficult to ignore the hard plastic between the seats, but the gear shift was darned annoying.

She wrapped one hand behind his head and flattened her other palm against his body, giving him slow caresses that made him suck in his breath. Teasing touches beneath his shirt to feel the smooth skin over hard muscle there. Combing through the soft hair in the center of his chest then down. Pressing against the zipper of his pants, which was currently strained to its limit.

He grasped her hand and held it motionless and tight in his. "You trying to make me wreck the car?"

"No. Just trying to hurry things up." She pressed closer against his shoulder, ignoring the stupid gear shift digging into her thigh. She sucked gently on his throat, every sense tuned to his scent and his taste and the feel of his skin.

"I do have to actually change gears, Dani." His voice was a low growl. "Please move over for just one minute. We're almost there."

Oh, right. The gear shift wasn't just an in-the-way annoyance. "Sorry." She straddled his lap and the bounce of the car on the rutted road pushed his hard erection right where she wanted it. The sensation was so erotic, she moaned. She tunneled her fingers into the thick, soft hair she loved to touch and very nearly gave him a full mouth-to-mouth kiss, but figured that wasn't compatible with him actually being able to see and drive.

"God, Dani." He gave a breathless laugh. "If you wiggle against me one more time, I'm gonna run off the road into a tree. Do you have some kind of death wish?"

"No." She knew the man could practically drive in his sleep. "Just remembering how much fun we had in Honduras. How crazy you made me back then. How crazy you make me now."

"You're crazy, all right. But I like it."

The car suddenly veered to the right and

bounced even more for another thirty feet or so before coming to a jarring stop.

Immediately, his arms wrapped around her, and the kisses between them became frenzied, their bodies rubbing together until Dani thought she might come undone with all her clothes still on.

Chase yanked his mouth from hers, and their panting breaths mingled in the air between them. His eyes glittered in the darkness. "I didn't drive all the way out here to make love to you against the damned steering-wheel. Come with me."

"I just about did."

His quiet laugh filled the car before he shoved open the door. Still holding her in his arms with her legs wrapped around his hips, he somehow managed to grab thick blankets from the backseat and stride with her toward a small cluster of trees.

She quit nibbling his face and neck to see where they were going. Probably would be a good idea to help with the blankets instead of just hanging onto him like a baboon.

She slid her legs off his hips and wasn't sure she could actually stand up. "Give me one."

Together, they laid the blankets over whatever spongy, soft, and dark plant life was thriving beneath the trees. "What is this stuff?"

"I don't know. Don't care either, except that the minute I saw it, I thought of lying here with you, watching the stars."

"I didn't know you'd gone anywhere since I've been here."

"I haven't."

His eyes, shining in the darkness, were filled with both desire and tenderness, and his meaning finally sank in. "You mean, you thought of me even before I showed up in Benin?" she whispered.

"Thought of you. Wondered about you. Dreamed of you."

His quiet voice slipped inside her heart until it felt so full, it was hard to breathe. He reached for her, held her close, and for a moment the heady sexual desire that had consumed them earlier gave way to a quiet, aching connection. To what they'd had before.

To what they still had now.

He loosened her hair from its band. Pulled off

her shirt between kisses. Caressed her collarbone, her shoulders, her back as he slipped off her bra. Pleasured her breasts with his mouth as he pushed off the rest of her clothes.

Then it was her turn. But she couldn't go slowly, as he had. His kisses, his touch had ignited the smoldering fire he'd lit within her earlier, and she made quick work of his clothes until they were both naked, with the cool night air skating across their skin.

She pushed him down onto the blanket and looked into his handsome face. At his shining eyes and sensual lips curved in a smile.

"You make me think of a wood nymph up there, naked and beautiful with your curly hair shining in the dark." His big hands slid up her thighs and his thumbs slipped into the juncture between them, stroking her slick skin until she gasped with pleasure.

"If I recall my mythology, Greek gods liked to play with wood nymphs. Are you a Greek god?" She said it teasingly, breathlessly, but it was, oh, so true that he looked like one, with his gorgeous, muscular physique, his dark hair, his eyes flecked with gold, and the kissable shape of his beautiful lips.

"If I need to be to play with you, the answer is yes," he said on a heavy breath, smiling. "Playing with you is my number-one fantasy."

"Good. Because I'm liking being a wood nymph. Playing with my Greek god." She slowly moved against his talented fingers, the tension coiling and rising deep inside. She ran her hands slowly over his chest, his shoulders, his arms, loving the feel of his skin, the breeze touching her body, the moonlight dancing across his face, his skin, his hair.

"I'm liking it, too." That smile still played about his lips. "It was worth nearly ending up in a ditch as we drove here."

She had to kiss those sensual, smiling lips and leaned over to cover his mouth with hers, slipping her tongue gently inside to touch his. He tasted so good, so wonderful, his skin so warm against hers, his chest hair tickling her sensitive breasts, she wanted to just stay there, draped over him, kissing him in the moonlight. Making up for all the lonely nights she'd missed his moist lips, his warm body, the shivery touch of his hands.

But the slow circles he was making with his thumbs turned her insides to a liquid fever and the fact that he was naked and right there wouldn't let her draw out the moment any longer. She rose up to sheath him with her wet heat, and the throaty groan he gave in response made her move faster, more urgently. His hands grasped her hips as he moved with her, their gazes locked.

"Dani." His voice a harsh whisper, he suddenly bent at the waist and took her into his arms, reversing their position so she lay beneath him. Their pace quickened, the night air filling with the sounds of their pleasure. His hands were everywhere, gently squeezing, caressing, holding her close, their mouths and bodies joined in a dance that took her back to every achingly beautiful day they'd shared deeply hidden in the mountains of Honduras.

"Dani," he said again against her mouth. She heard herself crying out against his lips, and he joined her with a groan that came deep from within his chest and reverberated within her own.

They lay there for a long time, their breathing slowly returning to normal. The feel of his face buried in her neck, the weight of his body pressing hers into the spongy mattress, his hand cupping her breast, was perfection.

Cool air slipped between them as he shifted, lying just off her, skin still pressed to skin. His finger slipped across her ribs to trace lazy circles on her stomach.

"I want you to know I'm planning to stay in Benin for my vacation time until I leave for Panama." He paused. "If that's okay with you."

"That would be good." Drew would get to spend even more time with Chase if he wasn't working. And she'd have a little while to make sense of all her confusion about the future.

He propped himself on one elbow, his face close to hers. He splayed his big hand over her navel as he looked down into her eyes. "About my wanting you to marry me—"

She pressed her fingers to his lips. "I thought we weren't going to talk about that. I just want to lie here with you and look at the stars. After the next couple weeks, we'll…figure out what's best for everyone."

"I'm not asking for an answer right now. I can wait. But there's something I need to say." His dark eyes had lost their sensual glow and were now deeply serious. "I'm sorry I was so…unpleasant when I said, back in Honduras, that I never wanted to get married and have kids. If I'd known about Drew, you know my answer would have been different."

A sharp pinch twisted her heart as she stared at his somber face. Was that supposed to make her feel happy? What did he want her to say in response? She already knew that was the only reason he wanted to marry her now.

She turned her face to look at the stars, their twinkling points blurring as unwelcome tears stung her eyes. The last thing she wanted was for Chase to see her all teary over him. To feel guilty that, even though he'd said he loved her back in Honduras, he hadn't loved her quite enough.

"It's all right. I understand."

"I haven't finished." He gently grasped her chin between his thumb and forefinger and brought her gaze back to his. "The reason I acted like such a jerk was because it crushed me to realize it was about to be over between us. I knew I couldn't live a regular, suburban life in the States. I couldn't be the husband you wanted and give you the family you wanted. And that hurt like hell."

She pressed her palms to his chest, feeling his heart beat strong and steady. "I figured you were the kind of guy who just wanted to be free. That I wasn't enough to make you think otherwise."

"Not enough?" He cupped her head between his hands and kissed her hard, as though she'd made him angry. When he broke the kiss, he looked down at her with disbelief etched on his face. "Too much. More than I deserved. A woman who was everything—a caring doctor who made everyone around her smile, a woman with an adventurous spirit, a woman any man would be damned lucky to have in his life. And on top of all that, so beautiful you made my chest ache every time I looked at you."

His eyes seemed to look deep into her heart. "I love you, Dani. You're everything I've ever wanted in a woman. And now you've given me Drew. He's a miracle I didn't think I could have in my life, but a miracle I can't imagine being without now."

Her throat closed and she wrapped her arms around his neck to give him a kiss she hoped showed him how much his words had moved her. How much they'd given her hope that a good life for the three of them really might be possible.

Their lips separated, and the emotion shimmering between the two of them caught her breath and expanded in her heart. The clear night, the fragrant air, the softness beneath their blanket, all wrapped them in a quiet intimacy neither wanted to have end just yet.

Chase settled back to lie flat next to her, shoulder to shoulder, fingers curled together as they stared at the stars.

CHAPTER FOURTEEN

DANI FINALLY BROKE the long, relaxed silence. "I'm always amazed at how the Big Dipper looks just the same here as in the States and Honduras," she said, trying to lead up to the conversation they needed to have about Brady.

He chuckled. "Yeah, amazing, Miss Astronomy. Remind me to not have you teaching Drew about physical science."

She playfully swatted him. "You know what I mean. That the world, really, is such a small orb in all of the universe, with billions of people floating together through space."

"Yeah."

She turned her head to look at him. "Your mom told me about Brady."

Silence again stretched between them, this time no longer calm and relaxed. The sound of his heavy sigh mingled with the chirp of crickets until he finally spoke. "Because we moved so much, Brady and I were best friends. We did everything together, even when we made friends with local kids and kids of other doctors and med professionals."

"I never had a brother or sister, and always wished I did." She squeezed his hand. "I can't imagine how hard it was for you to lose him."

"Yeah. One minute he was with us, the next he was gone."

He turned his head toward her, the softness that had been in his eyes earlier now gone. Replaced by the hard and determined stare she'd become accustomed to when he objected to Andrew being in Africa.

"Now you understand why Drew can't live here. Why, short term, Panama would be safer. Why it's best for the two of you to live in the States until he wouldn't be as susceptible to a serious illness."

"So you'd be okay with our living there and you living here, or in Central America, or in India?" Trying to wrap her brain around how that would work was hard. But his mission work was such a big part of his life, it would be wrong to ask him to give it up completely. Even if he did, he'd ultimately resent it, and very likely Drew would sense that resentment.

Could she give up her desire to do mission work, too? Was it fair of him to even ask? Or perhaps she could convince Chase to compromise, every few years working together in somewhat safer locations like Panama.

"I'd be in the U.S. several months a year." His fingers tightened on hers and his breath brushed her cheek. "It's not a perfect solution, but I know we can make it work."

Could they? Just hours ago she'd been sure the answer was a resounding "No." But maybe, just maybe, an imperfect solution could still be the best solution.

"Now you know about Brady. It's your turn," he said, rolling onto his side, head propped on his hand, his fingers sliding across her stomach again. "You said something about knowing what it's like to have a parent think you're a burden. Why?"

"My parents were college sweethearts. Dad was

the only child of a well-to-do family. Apparently there were expectations that he'd concentrate on school, get an MBA and eventually take over the family business."

He touched his lips to her shoulder. "And?"

"Mom got pregnant. And that didn't fit into anyone's plans. They didn't get married, but his family's lawyers set up child support. Which wasn't much because, at that time he was just a student and the court didn't factor in his family's money."

"And he never had much to do with you?"

"No." She shook her head, surprised that, even now, she felt a sliver of hurt over it. "He complained to her all the time about any extra expenses she asked for help with. Sometimes plain refused. When Mom tried to get him to talk to me on the phone, he was curt and got off as fast as possible."

"Did he pay the child support?"

"Oh, he dutifully sent the checks, and his parents even paid for part of my med-school tuition. Which they didn't have to do, and I was grateful for it." His hand moved to cup her ribs and she turned her head to look at him. "But every time I invited them to some school event, they came up with an excuse. Said they were too busy. He married somebody in his social sphere, but never had kids. He and his wife travelled all over the world. Still do, I suppose."

Enough with the self-pity, which was absurd after all these years. She lightened her tone. "Hard to believe I never even got the souvenir shirt that said 'My dad went to Paris but all I got was this lousy T.'"

"So you felt unwanted and unloved by him and that felt like crap. I get why you've been so worried Drew would feel the same way." He cupped her face in his hand, his dark eyes earnest. "You do know I'll always be here for both of you, don't you? Always."

She did know. The man was the most honorable and caring person she'd ever met. "Yes. And if we decide—"

"Uh-uh." He rolled onto her, pinned her beneath him, pulled her hands above her head and silenced her with a kiss. "I know I've been pushing you hard for an answer, but now I'm pulling back. Giving you three weeks before we talk about it at all. Then we'll come back here and have this conversation again."

"Just the conversation?"

His teeth were white in the darkness as he grinned, pressing his body into hers as they sank deeper into the spongy earth. "Well, you know what they say about all talk and no action…"

With the sun barely peeking through the curtains, Dani couldn't believe how wide awake she felt. As she stretched, she had to smile at the little aches and twinges from the previous evening's physical activities.

She rolled over and closed her eyes to try to get another hour of sleep. After ten minutes or so it was very apparent that wasn't happening. She stood and pulled on sweats and a T-shirt and peeked at Drew. His sweet lips were parted as he slept soundly and she kissed his head before creeping out the door to make some coffee.

As she expected, the kitchen was quiet and empty, but to her surprise the delicious scent of coffee filled the room. Early-bird Chase must have made it before his run and workout.

Perhaps he was finished and already in the shower. The thought of finding out and joining him there was more than tempting and she walked down the hall to peek into the shower room.

Darn. Dark and quiet. She smirked at the disappointment she felt. Since when had she become a sex maniac?

She knew the answer. Since being with Chase again.

It was hard to believe an entire week had gone by since his parents had left. A week of fulfilling work and lovely family time. Not to mention all those close and intimate moments with Chase after Drew was asleep.

In mere days the man had managed to make her fall headlong in love with him again. Or maybe the truth was she'd stayed in love with him all this time. In love with his strengths and his commitment to others and those deep brown eyes she sank into every time she looked at him.

And, of course, she loved his knee-weakening kisses. The thought sent her mind back to the shower and the fact that he must still be out running and would need one when he returned. Her heart did a little pit-pat, and it was clear she needed a distraction from her libido. A vibrant sunrise peeked through the window, and she wandered outside to enjoy it.

Streaked gray clouds stood out against a magenta sky, the bright orange ball of the sun casting, as it rose above the horizon, a beautiful pink glow across the savannah. She took a sip of her coffee, letting the taste linger on her tongue, then nearly choked as a movement by a nearby tree startled her.

Chase. Doing rapid push-ups like he was in an army boot camp. Doubtless he'd already been for his run and was engrossed in the rest of his fitness regimen. Thank heavens he hadn't dragged her out of bed to join him. Next would come squats and lunges and some kind of upper-body work, and he was the worst drill sergeant ever, with no sympathy for anyone's tired muscles. Not to mention that Chase had given her muscles a very good workout last night.

His biceps bulged and deltoids rippled and just as Dani was admiring all those manly muscles, he jumped up and ran to a tree, leaping to grasp the lowest branch to start on pull-ups.

She'd almost forgotten how beautiful his body was. Even during their lovemaking, when she'd seen him naked, run her hands over his solid strength, she'd been so focused on other things she hadn't taken the time to admire him, which had been pretty much her favorite hobby in Honduras.

But now, with the vivid sun silhouetting his wide, muscular shoulders, his powerful chest, his strong thighs, she let her eyes savor him. It was all she could do not to walk over and slip her hands beneath his T-shirt, currently hiking up with each movement to expose his belly button and the line of dark hair on his taut stomach. To feel his smooth skin all slippery from sweat.

Thinking about that made her feel very warm, like she was the one doing all those pull-ups. Better get back inside before she couldn't resist dragging him into the shower or back to bed, which wasn't a good idea with Drew waking up soon. Or before Chase spotted her and made her hit the ground for push-ups and sit-ups of her own.

Now, there was an alarming thought. She backed towards the door, turning to escape.

"Running away scared?"

She looked over her shoulder as he dropped to the ground and walked towards her in that easy, athletic stride of his.

"No. I'm not afraid of your workouts. You can put me to the test any time." Which he'd done last night. And the night before. Unable to resist his seductive and convincing kisses, she'd completely failed every test. Or aced them, she thought with an inward smile.

"Yeah?" He stopped in front of her and pulled her into his arms. Warm brown eyes smiled into hers before his lips slipped across hers, feather soft.

With his arm draped across her shoulders, they walked together to the kitchen, and Chase poured more coffee into her cup.

"Thanks for making coffee. You sure know the way to a girl's heart."

"I know a few other ways, too."

"You do?" The way he looked at her, the smile on his beautiful lips, had her leaning in for a kiss, stroking her hand down his damp shirt and over the bulging front of his shorts.

"Is that all you think about?" he teased, his voice a low growl. He picked up a covered plate from the counter and slid the foil off. "I was referring to Ruth's coffee cake."

"Well, that is another way to my heart." The cake did smell delicious, but not quite as delicious as Chase.

"I'm thinking this earns me double points," he said.

"It does." She pinched a piece and stuck it in her mouth. "Definitely. So what do you want to use your points for?"

He pulled her close for a kiss, lips clinging before he pulled back, the corners of his eyes crinkled, his lips teasingly curved. She could get used to waking up to this. To the taste of warm coffee and Chase on her tongue.

She poked another piece of cake into her mouth and Chase licked a crumb from her lips. "I'm thinking my points should get me—"

The kitchen door swung open and Trent walked in then slapped his hand over his eyes. "Could you two please keep your romantic moments out of the public areas of the compound? I'm afraid to go anywhere now for fear of having my innocence corrupted."

"Your innocence was corrupted long, long ago, Casanova," Chase said. He moved to the counter and poured a cup of coffee, handing it to Trent. "When are you leaving for your vacation?"

"In about an hour. I'm meeting a friend in Brussels, and we're going to do a little European tour for a few weeks."

"Would this friend be of the female persuasion?" Chase asked.

"Of course." Trent swigged some coffee and rocked back on his heels. "What would be the point of spending a few weeks with a man? Working with you for the past year has been torture enough."

Dani laughed. She'd heard about Trent's reputation, and wondered how much of it was really true. "I hope you have a great time. And that you enjoy your stint in India."

"Thanks." He turned to Chase and reached to shake his hand. "God knows why, but in all seriousness I'll miss you. I hope we work together next time around."

"Me, too."

They smiled at one another with an obviously close bond forged between two doctors who spent their lives doing what so few others did. As difficult as it would be to pull up roots and start somewhere new every year, part of Dani envied their amazing commitment.

"Good thing you're spending your vacation here as I hear the only doc coming to replace both of us is going to be a week or so late," Trent said.

"Yeah. Think they'll give me double pay for working through my vacation?"

"You'll be lucky if they don't pay you in goats and yams."

Both men grinned, and Trent set his coffee on the table to give Dani a warm hug. "You take care of Drew and keep me posted on how he's doing. And best of luck with this one." He jabbed his thumb towards Chase. "Because you're definitely going to need a lot of luck."

"Thanks. I know." She looked over at Chase's smile, her heart lifting with a sweet ache, and knew she already had a whole lot of luck in her pocket.

Trent left, and Chase pulled her close for another quick kiss. "Tomorrow we'll be busy, with just the two of us here. What do you think about taking Drew back to the hotel today to swim and have lunch? I've got a taste for the burgers they serve there."

"Sounds perfect."

His hands drifted down to cup her rear. "I need a shower. Feel like joining me?"

"If Drew's still asleep, we can—"

He grabbed her hand and practically pulled her out of her shoes as he hurried her down the hall. "I'm ready to redeem my double points. Like right now."

Dani took the last swig of her iced tea and chuckled as she watched Chase and Drew play in the hotel pool. They'd been at it for hours, with only short breaks, and she knew their son would sleep very well tonight.

"And then Superman swoops into the ocean to save Metropolis!"

Chase held Drew's small body between his hands as he dove him headfirst into the water and back up to the surface.

"Again!" Drew swiped his hair and the pool water from his eyes, his grin nearly stretching from one ear to the other. She hadn't realized until she'd seen him all wet how much the child needed a haircut, and made a note to do that tomorrow after work.

She had to laugh at the way Drew held his arms stiffly at his sides like the true Superman, and at Chase's silly comic-book commentary. How amazing that the child who had never liked water being poured over his head to rinse out shampoo now adored being completely underwater. He even liked to jump straight in from the side of the pool, as long as his daddy was there to catch him.

Chase was so good with him that she felt ashamed that she'd ever believed he'd be a distant dad. Yes, there would be physical distance while Chase worked overseas, but Drew would always know how much his daddy loved him, of that she no longer had any doubt.

A few other women sipping drinks by the pool

barely concealed the way they eyed Chase, and who could blame them? With his handsome face and bronzed skin over all that muscle, he truly looked like the Greek god she'd teased him about being when they'd made love outside in the moonlight. And he could be…was…all hers.

She stood and walked to the side of the pool. "It's four o'clock, you two. We need to be leaving pretty soon."

"I not done saving Metroplis," Drew said. "Mommy, watch me dive!"

"All right, Superman. Here we go again." Chase grinned at Dani and readjusted his hands on a wriggling Drew before he dunked him beneath the water again.

The grin on Chase's face suddenly died, replaced by a deep frown. He started wading toward the shallowest water, holding Drew up against his chest.

"I not done swimming, Daddy."

"I know. I just want to check something."

The odd expression on Chase's face set off an alarm in Dani's brain. Something was worrying him, and he wasn't a man prone to worry.

Dani's feet landed on the top step of the pool just as Chase stood Drew there. "What's wrong?" she asked.

Frowning, he began to palpate Drew's abdomen, but the child leaped, trying to jump back into the pool. Chase moved his hands to grip Drew's arms and brought his face close to their son's. "Hold still, Superman. I want to see if you've got kryptonite in your belly."

Drew's eyes lit up at the idea. "Okay."

Dani's heart began to thud and her breath grew short. Why, exactly, she didn't know, but something about the way Chase looked made her feel very, very uneasy. She stepped farther down into the pool next to him and leaned close to Chase, staring as he pressed his fingers gently but firmly into Drew's abdomen and flank.

"What's the matter, Chase?"

He turned to look at her, and his shaken expression, the starkness in his eyes closed her throat. His chest lifted as he sucked in a deep breath before turning back to Drew. "Superman, the kryptonite is going to make you unable to move. Why don't you go up and sit in the chair to finish your smoothie. That'll melt the kryptonite and you'll be strong again."

"Okay. I need to get strong!" Drew grinned and hurried up the steps to grab his drink and sit in the chair.

Dani grabbed Chase's arm. "You're scaring me. What's wrong?"

He closed his eyes for a moment and scrubbed his hand across his face. When he looked down at her, his gaze was tortured. "There's a large mass inside his belly. With its location and his age, my best guess would be nephroblastoma. Wilm's tumor."

"Oh, my God. No," she whispered. Her heart stopped completely. "No. He couldn't possibly have cancer."

CHAPTER FIFTEEN

CHASE PLACED THE X-ray cartridge beneath Drew's lower back and swiveled the C-arm of the machine over his mid-section, trying to stay calm and professional. The moment he'd touched that hard mass inside Drew's little body he'd felt like someone had kicked in his chest and stopped his heart, and only the fact that he'd taken and developed X-rays hundreds of times enabled him to function at all.

"Okay, Superman? We're going to take some pictures of that kryptonite in there."

"Okay, Daddy."

His son's huge grin made Chase's throat close. He didn't know how the hell he could manage to keep acting like this was all a big game, but somehow he had to stay strong. Had to make sure he didn't scare Drew by showing the gut-wrenching terror that made it hard to breathe.

"After we take the pictures, Mommy's going to fix you your favorite dinner," Dani said. Chase glanced at her as she held Drew's hand and knew she couldn't possibly be holding up any better than he was. The strain and fear on her face made her look suddenly older, and she stared at him in mute anguish.

The car ride back from the hotel had been quiet. Despite Drew falling asleep in his car seat, Chase and Dani hadn't said much. What the hell was there to say? They didn't know anything yet. Didn't know if it was Wilm's tumor or something else. Something non-malignant. Or something even worse than Wilm's.

The shock of it had left both of them stunned and speechless. He hoped to God the X-ray would give them some idea what they were dealing with, but he had a bad feeling they wouldn't know much more than they did now.

"That's it, Superman." Chase pulled out the cartridge and swung the C-arm away. He lifted Drew's small body into his arms and held him tightly against him, closing his eyes for a moment and trying to slow his breathing. Calm his tripping heart.

He headed into the kitchen with the child. "Let's get you something to eat. Your mom will fix your dinner while I get the pictures developed. It'll be important for you to eat good food to build all your muscles."

Drew snaked his arms around Chase's neck. "I will, Daddy. I getting big muscles like you."

Chase sat his son on a kitchen stool and ruffled his hair, somehow managing to force a smile. He turned to Dani, who was busying herself putting together Drew's meal.

"I'll ask Spud to sit with him while he's eating," he said to Dani. "Give me time to get the X-rays developed then come down to the clinic."

She nodded without speaking, without even looking at him, and he headed off and spoke briefly with Spud. Desperately anxious to see what the X-rays showed, he dreaded what they might indicate.

He shoved the films up into the old light box hanging on the wall and peered at them. What he saw made him sway slightly on his feet, unable to catch his breath. It took a Herculean effort to stay upright instead of slumping down into a chair, and he was leaning his hand against the wall to support himself when Dani walked in.

"What do they look like?" she asked, her voice barely above a whisper.

"See the shadow?" He grasped her arm, tugged her closer to look at the films. "There's a suggestion of a large mass in his left flank. Whatever it is, it's big. I'm guessing at least a pound. From what I can see, though, it doesn't look like it's metastasized into the lungs."

"Oh, God." She stared at the films, and tears filled her eyes and spilled over. "Can you take it out?"

"If this was a kid who lived here, whose life was here, I'd do what I had to do." If Dani hadn't been so naive, so damned carefree, they wouldn't be in this situation. "But who knows what the hell it is for sure? We don't have CAT scans and MRIs and ultrasound. We can't even do a biopsy unless we take him to Cotonou."

"I think we should take him to Cotonou right away."

"Are you crazy?" He stared at her and wondered if she was denying the reality staring them both in the face. "We have to make a plan, this second, to get him to the States for a complete diagnosis. Then surgery by someone who knows exactly what they're doing. And chemo, which he'll probably need."

"Maybe it's not malignant. Maybe it's just a benign tumor."

"Maybe. Are you willing to take that chance? Apparently you like taking chances, as you brought him here in the first place. But I'm not willing to take that chance, because you know as well as I do what these X-rays indicate. That it's a pipe dream to hope it's not Wilm's or some other cancer."

The dread and anger he'd been shoving down for hours welled up in his chest and burst out in words he knew he shouldn't say. Words he couldn't stop. "If you hadn't brought him here, like I said all along you shouldn't have, he could already be in a hospital in the States. But, no, he's here in Africa. And it's going to take days to make that happen."

He jabbed his finger at the image of the mass inside their baby's body. "And if it *is* Wilm's, you also know how fast it grows. How it can metastasize practically overnight."

Tortured-looking watery blue eyes stared at him. "Are you blaming me for this? I love him more than anything in the world." A sob caught in her throat and she pressed the back of her hand to her mouth.

"That love should have told you to do everything in your power to keep him safe. But instead you brought a two-year-old to a developing country."

"You *are* blaming me," she said, anguish and disbelief choking her voice. "He obviously had this before we even left the States. Neither you or I could have protected him from something like this."

"No." He grabbed the films from the light box and shoved them in a folder. "But if you'd kept him where he belongs, Drew would be getting the necessary tests done right this minute. Getting treatment that could very well mean the difference between a good outcome and a bad one."

He slammed his hand against the cement wall, unable to control the fury that kept welling up in his chest, twisting with the icy fear lodged there. "Between life and death."

Dani burst into tears and buried her face in her hands.

Damn it, he shouldn't have yelled at her. But she also needed to hear it. Had to know he was right. Had to know she could never put Drew in a dangerous situation like this again.

He sucked in several breaths before trying to speak again. "What's the best children's hospital near where you live in the States?"

"I rented out my house, so we can't stay there. We can choose any hospital anywhere and just stay at a hotel."

"You're the one who knows the best pediatric cancer hospitals in the U.S. Decide on one, make some calls, and I'll get the plane tickets and other arrangements taken care of."

"And I guess I need to call GPC. Try to get someone here to take my place."

"Somebody needs to be available in the clinic until the new doc gets here and knows what he's doing." The thought of not being able to go with them immediately tore at Chase's heart, but they couldn't just leave the clinic empty. Who knew what desperate patient might walk through the door? "I'll take your place here until I can leave."

"You aren't coming with us?"

The shock in her eyes added to the heavy weight in his chest, but there was no way around it. "You know the new doc isn't coming for another week or so. I can't leave the place with absolutely no one here. But I'll come as soon as I can."

Myriad emotions flitted through her eyes as she searched his face. He wasn't sure what all he saw etched there, but sad and weary disillusionment seemed to shadow her eyes. She nodded and turned away.

"I'll make some calls. Hopefully Drew and I will be out of here by tomorrow."

At the Philadelphia children's hospital, Dani sat alone in the harshly lit waiting room as her son underwent surgery to remove the huge tumor growing inside his small body. She'd kissed Drew as he'd sat in the rolling crib they used to take him to the OR, his little face smiling as though he was on a great adventure, and it had taken all her strength to smile back, to wave as if he was heading off to a play date.

The moment he'd disappeared from sight the tears had begun. Flowing from deep within her soul in what felt like an endless reservoir of dread. She thought of the poor mother bleeding to death whose life Chase had saved, and felt a little like that. That she just might slowly die if she lost her baby boy. Intellectually, she knew life would go on. But it would be forever altered.

She flipped through the battered magazines, but gave up on being able to read anything. So strange to be sitting out in this room with other parents and the siblings of patients instead of on the other side of the wall, involved in a patient's care. Absently, she watched little ones play with the toys in the room, loud and giggling, munching on snacks from little plastic bags and reading stories with their parents, completely unaware of what their families were going through.

Of course, some of the surgeries going on that

moment were fairly routine, with little risk. But others? Heart surgeries and brain surgeries.

Cancer treatments.

She leaned her head against the wall and closed her eyes. Never, in her worst nightmares, would she ever have thought Drew would have to go through something like this. She tried hard to re-member that Wilm's tumor, if that was what he had, was highly treatable. That over eighty-five percent of children survived it. Thrived, healthy and happy, the rest of their lives. And she prayed hard, over and over, that Drew would be one of them.

She shoved herself from the chair to grab a cup of coffee from the smiling, elderly volun-teer pushing a cart with beverages and snacks. She moved slowly to the rain-spattered window, staring outside at the gray sky, and wondered if the sun was shining in Benin.

She'd forgiven Chase for being so angry with her. For somehow blaming her. He loved Drew nearly as much as she did, and she knew his out-burst, his agitation had stemmed from the same shock and terror she'd felt. People did and said things under stress they normally wouldn't.

She'd even forgiven him for not coming back to the States with them. Or maybe forgiven was the wrong word. Accepted, painfully, what she'd known all along but had buried beneath her love for him. Beneath her desire to believe they could have a future together, however complicated.

His work was his life. Who he was. Without it, he wouldn't have an identity that he understood, and that identity took precedence over everything.

But, as bewildered as she felt, one thing became very clear. As she'd taken Drew to his first doctor's appointments, to the first of so many tests, when she'd held his hand as he'd cried during the MRI, and as he'd been poked and pinched as his blood had been drawn, she'd known the life Chase proposed for them wasn't enough.

For a short time, in his arms, through his kisses, she'd become convinced it was, and just thinking about those moments filled her with a deep longing. But through all the lonely hours since she'd brought Drew back to the States, she'd come to see that she deserved more.

She deserved a husband who would be with her every day. Through good times and bad times. In sickness and in health, as the marriage vows said. And that simply wasn't possible with him living across the world most of every year.

She rested her forehead against the cold pane of glass. She loved Chase. Loved him so much it hurt. But many of the things she loved about him were the same things that drove him to do the work he did.

He couldn't change who he was, and she couldn't even really want him to, because he was like no one else she'd ever known. A man with so much to offer humankind but not enough to offer her.

"I know this cast feels even worse than the last one, but at least you don't have to deal with that apparatus any more, right?"

Chase leaned over Apollo and checked the new cast he'd put on the boy, which extended over his whole leg now that the boy's wound had healed enough to be covered. "Does it hurt?"

The boy shook his head and smiled. "The 'be happy' song makes it better."

Don't worry, be happy. Chase swallowed hard. That wasn't even close to possible.

Apollo's mother reached under the blankets she had stacked next to the bed and brought out a small fetish she'd most likely made herself, handing it to Chase. "I heard the pretty doctor's son was sick and needed to go back to America," she said. "I wish to give this to her and her son, asking for Sakpata's healing."

Her son. His son.

"Thank you. I'll let her know." Chase took the beaded and painted mud statue from the woman and tried to smile. If only such a thing could really help. But Drew's health—his survival—would come down to modern medicine and a little luck.

Each time he'd treated small children in the clinic, their faces had blurred to look like Drew's. His big brown eyes and his beautiful smile. And through every crisis, every surgery he hadn't been able to take his mind off him for even a second. Wondering how he was doing. What he was going through. If he'd be okay.

Wondering how Dani was holding up through it all.

Chase moved on to the next patient, thinking about his last phone call with Dani. She'd given him the details of Drew's tests, what they showed, what they planned to do. Her voice had sounded calm, her recitation to the point. She sounded okay, but he suspected it was an act. His frustration level at not being able to be there with them threatened to make it nearly impossible for him to focus on his work.

When the hell was the new doctor going to get here?

His cellphone rang and he pulled it from his pocket. His mother. Calling for at least the tenth time.

"I'm wondering if there's any news."

Her voice reflected the same tightly controlled foreboding he felt that had every nerve on alert. "No, Mom. She said she'd call after the tumor was removed. After they do a biopsy to confirm the diagnosis."

"I still think you need to go be with them, Chase. I think you should book your flight."

"I can't do that yet." Surely she knew he felt as frustrated and anxious as she did? But she also knew that if he left there wouldn't be one damned person here to take care of an emergency. And the nurses would have to take care of the hospital patients alone, with a few in serious condition.

"You do know it's okay to put yourself first once in a while, don't you? You need to be there to support Dani through all this."

"It isn't logical for me to go there where there are umpteen doctors of all specialties ready to take care of Drew, and not a single doctor here to take care of these people. You know that."

"That's not really true, Chase. That hospital has their techs who are well trained for things like hernia surgery, and they'd do the best they could if there wasn't a doctor there." His mother's voice grew more irritated, which he rarely heard from her. "You have your whole life to take care of needy people in the world; you have only this moment to take care of Dani and your son."

He stared at the hospital ward, at all the sick and injured patients, and didn't know what the hell to think. How could he abandon them? Yes, the techs could handle most problems if necessary, but it felt…wrong to leave them without a truly qualified surgeon. And yet the place he wanted to be was with Dani and Drew.

He hung up and pulled out his stethoscope to check the next patient.

"The prognosis is very good, Dr. Sheridan." The surgeon, still wearing his blue cap and surgical gown, sat in the chair next to hers in the waiting room. "I suspect it was, indeed, a Wilm's tumor, but of course we'll have to wait for the biopsy results to confirm that. It was a stage-one tumor, completely isolated in one kidney. With the removal of the tumor, kidney, and ureter, I think only a short course of chemotherapy will be necessary. He's going to be fine."

Dani nearly slid off the chair at his words, tears clogging her throat. Her first thought was to wonder if Drew was awake and wanting her. Her next thought was that she wished Chase was there to embrace in shared relief.

"Can I see him now?"

"He's in Recovery. Still asleep, but you can go on in there so he'll see you when he first wakes up." The doctor smiled and patted her shoulder. "We'll keep him in the hospital a couple of days. Then we'll discuss the next step."

The nurse led her to Recovery and she sat next to Drew, holding his hand, knowing he'd be in pain and maybe confused when he awoke. She'd brought a pillow and blanket to spread on the narrow, but thankfully padded, window seat in his room so she would be right there for him if he needed her.

His eyelids fluttered and he looked up at her. "Mommy?"

"I'm right here, sweetheart." As she squeezed his hand, her own heart squeezed until she thought it might burst wide open. While she knew there was still a slim chance something could go wrong, it sounded like they'd been very, very lucky.

She slowly combed her fingers through his

beautiful, thick hair, her heart clutching at the thought that it might all fall out during chemo. She couldn't even imagine it, but would figure out a way to make it seem okay, maybe even fun. After all, he was still so little he might like the adventure of using his noggin as a canvas for non-toxic markers, and managed a smile at the silly thought.

"Is Daddy here?" he asked, his voice sleepy and slurred.

"Not yet." And wasn't that what she'd probably be telling him his whole life? That his daddy would be home whenever he could be there? Maybe soon? Or, more likely, not soon at all.

Tears yet again closed her throat, slipped from her eyes to sting her cheeks, as she told herself it would be all right. It had to be all right. Drew would recover and grow up to be a smart, strong and handsome man like his father. Chase would be there for him when he could be, talk to him a lot, probably send him photos via computer of all the places he was living and all the things he was doing.

And she would be right here for Drew. Every day.

* * *

Chase concentrated on his push-ups, trying to block everything else from his mind. Fifty-five. Fifty-six. Fifty-seven.

He never worked out twice in one day. The darkness that surrounded him was usually pre-dawn, not dusk. But he had to do something to deal with the anxious restlessness consuming him.

Dani had said she'd call once she knew any-thing. Hours and hours ago she'd promised that, but he hadn't heard a word. Kept checking his phone to be sure it was on, that its ringer was turned up, that he hadn't somehow missed her call.

He headed towards his favorite tree, which had lost a few limbs to storms but somehow survived. It stood scarred but still strong, and he leaped to grab the lowest branch. When the phone rang shrilly, he dropped to the ground and nearly fell on his face. Fumbling to snag it out of his pocket, he quickly hit the button.

"Hello? Dani, is that you?"

"Yes. It's me. I wanted to tell you he came out

of surgery okay and he's doing fine. It was stage one, so they're sure they got everything. And they expect the biopsy to confirm it was Wilm's, so the prognosis for a full recovery is really good."

His legs felt so weak they seemed to crumple beneath him as he sat on the ground. "Thank God." He swiped his hand across his face and moist eyes, not caring that dust covered his palm. "Are you doing okay?"

"I'm fine." Her voice was calm, cool. "I'll call you tomorrow to let you know how he's feeling."

"Wait." Was that it? She'd barely spoken with him and was going to hang up? "Can I talk to him?"

"He's finally back asleep. He was in a lot of pain and cranky, but they upped his pain meds and he's comfortable now. Oh, wait, he's crying a little again. I've got to go. I'll call you later."

The phone went dead in his ear and he stared at it. He should feel elated. *Did* feel relieved beyond belief that the tumor had been caught early and Drew would most likely recover completely.

But with that relief came overwhelming disquiet. As he sat there in the dirt, he looked up at the night sky.

He wished Dani was looking at it with him. Not from Philadelphia but from here.

No. He stared hard at the stars, shining steadily and brightly. It seemed he could almost see the slow turning of the earth, the stars growing more brilliant and defined as they rotated infinitesimally in the sky, and knew.

He should be looking at it in Philadelphia with her.

He scrambled up and dialed the airline. He hoped to God the new doc would show up tomorrow as he was supposed to. And prayed that the techs wouldn't have problems covering any emergency, if necessary. But right now, there was only one place in the world he belonged. He belonged with Dani and Drew.

"Come on, you have to eat more than that." Dani poked raisins into Drew's oatmeal to make another smiley face, hoping he'd eat a few of the oats along with the raisins he kept picking out.

"Dig out his whole eyeball with your spoon, and gobble it up like the monster you are."

"I not a monster. I a lizard, eating my bugs."

He picked out the raisins again, and Dani sighed. She needed to stop fussing over him, worrying about every bite of food. It was obvious he was feeling better every day, and she couldn't wait until this afternoon when he would get to go home.

"I brought some Benin bugs back for you, lizard-boy," a deep voice said.

Dani swung around and stared, her stomach feeling as if it was jumping up to lodge in her throat. There Chase stood, tall and strong, his brown eyes tired but intense, his entire form radiating energy. She wanted to run to him and throw her arms around him and beg him to never leave again.

"Daddy!" Drew shrieked and tried to scramble out of the bed, but Dani quickly put a restraining hand on his chest.

"You can't just leap out of bed with all this stuff attached to you," she said. "Lie still."

Chase came farther into the room and draped

his arm around Dani, pulling her close as he sat on the side of the bed. His eyes met hers, and a familiar ache filled her chest. He leaned forward to give her a soft kiss, and he tasted so good she forced herself to remember all the lonely days and nights and her conviction that she deserved more than he could offer.

Chase turned his attention to Drew, leaned down to kiss his cheek. He stroked one finger across the child's forehead to get his hair out of his eyes then cupped the side of Drew's head with his wide palm. But he kept Dani tugged close against him. "You've been through an awful lot, getting that kryptonite out of your belly, Superman. How are you feeling?"

"Okay. My tummy hurts but Mommy says it'll be better soon."

"I'm sorry it hurts. You're very brave, and I'm proud of you."

"Time to change his dressing," a nurse said with a smile as she walked in.

Chase stood, and Dani stood with him, because she didn't have a choice with his arm tight around her body. They took a few steps away from the bed to give the nurse room.

"I'd like to see the wound." Chase studied it carefully after the nurse had removed the dressing, then nodded in satisfaction. He smiled at Drew. "Looks good, buddy. Your mom and I'll be in the hall while the nurse gets you fixed up. We'll be right back."

Chase moved into the hallway, taking Dani with him, and in some ways she felt like she was right back where they'd been the first time they'd seen one another again in the sub-Saharan twilight. But this time she knew she would remember how much she'd missed him this week. She knew she could stay strong.

He drew her farther down the hall to a darkened nook holding a single chair. He slipped between the chair and wall and pulled her to him, looking down at her eyes, his own deeply serious.

"When did the new doctor arrive?" she asked.

"Thankfully, he showed up at the airport as I was about to leave."

"At the airport?" Had Chase left before the new

doctor was in place? She opened her mouth to ask but he pressed his fingers to her lips.

"Before you speak, I have some things I need to say." His hands moved to cup her face, his thumb slipping across her cheekbone. "I was looking at the night sky and saw the Big Dipper. And I thought about you saying that we're all spinning around together on this tiny speck in the universe called Earth. I realized I didn't want to be looking at the stars, knowing you're looking at them too, and not be with you, looking at them together."

Her eyes stung and her fingers curled into his shirt, but she didn't know what she was supposed to say. Didn't know exactly what he was saying.

He brushed her lips softly with his, and she wanted to kiss him longer, wanted to feel his mouth soothe away all the worries, all the loneliness.

"I always said being a mission doctor wasn't just what I did, but who I was." His breath touched her moist lips as he spoke. "I was wrong."

He tucked a strand of hair behind her ear, and she wanted to wrap her arms around him and hold him close. "How were you wrong?"

"It's not who I am. It's just what I do. Who I am is the man who loves you and wants to be with you and share my life with you. Who I am is Drew's father, and I want to share my life with him, too." He pulled her close and buried his face in her hair. "I love you for just you, and I love him for just him. I love you, and all I want is to share my life with both of you."

He looked at her again, and she knew he meant every word. That it wasn't just a brief reaction to the terrifying crisis of Drew's illness but words from deep within his heart.

"I love you, too," she whispered. "So much. But it scares you to have Drew live in the places you work."

"Which is why I'm staying here. Working here. With you. In whichever one of the fifty United States you choose. My mother pointed out that I—we—have the rest of our lives after Andrew grows bigger to work missions around the world. If you want to. Until then I'm sure I can find work here where I know I can make some kind of difference."

He drew her to the chair and gently sat her in it.

His eyes focused on hers, he held both her hands and slowly dropped to one knee. "I know I was pushy and demanding before, and I'm sorry for that. But I can't wait any longer for you to ask me again to marry you."

"Chase, I—"

"No, it's my turn now." His hands tightened on hers. "Will you marry me, Dani? I'll do anything you ask of me if you'll let me be a part of your life. And Drew's. On your terms, not mine. I'm asking you because I can't be complete without you. I'm begging you because I don't want to live without you. Please, will you marry me?"

"Oh, Chase. Yes. I will." She felt her mouth tremble in a wobbly smile. "I've missed you so much."

His chest lifted in a deep breath and he closed his eyes for a moment before looking at her with so much love her heart felt almost too full to hold it all.

"Thank you." He stood and pulled her into his arms, holding her close. "I missed you for three damned years and I'm not missing you again for even one more day."

He lowered his head and kissed her, and it was so warm and sweet it was like drinking in happiness.

She wrapped her arms around his neck and pressed her cheek to his. "We should probably go back to Drew's room. I get to take him home today. Except that, for the moment, home is a hotel."

"*We* get to take him back home today. And then we'll get started on figuring out where home's going to be."

With the promise of everything she'd ever wanted within his warm gaze, he took her hand and they walked down the hall to be with their son.

Together.

EPILOGUE

LAUGHTER ECHOED OFF the walls of their new home in Chicago as Drew put on a puppet show for his three doting grandparents. On his hand was a pink pig puppet that was dancing so frenetically he kept knocking down the wobbly, cardboard cutout they'd glued red fabric "curtains" to.

It had been so hard to decide where in the U.S. they should live, but Dani and Chase had finally decided on the Windy City. As Chicago was close to Dani's mother and offered a widely diverse population, they both found work here that they enjoyed, and it was a great place to raise Drew, too.

Along with another little one. Dani placed her hand on her belly to feel the hard kicks the baby kept jabbing into her stomach as she tried to watch Drew's show. Their unborn baby girl seemed to be dancing around as much as Drew's pig was, and Dani grinned at her husband. He grinned back, his lizard puppet making little kisses at her, complete with sound effects.

He turned the puppet toward Drew. "You have any bugs, little pink piggy? I love bugs! I'm gonna lick them up!"

Dani, her mother, and Chase's parents all laughed at the ridiculous falsetto voice he was using, as well as Drew's comical reaction to the lizard puppet licking and biting him all over.

Evelyn squeezed Dani's arm. "I'm so thrilled we decided to move here for a few years. Think how much we would have missed our Andrew. And our granddaughter too, whenever she decides to meet us."

"Hopefully, very soon," Dani said with a smile, getting up to walk stiffly—waddle was probably a more accurate word—to pour herself decaffeinated coffee and place four candles on Andrew's birthday cake.

"I would have gotten that for you, honey," her mother Sandra, said, rising to busy herself gathering plates from the kitchen. Amazingly, Chase's parents were now employed at the same hospital where Dani's mother worked as a nurse. Unbelievable that a family that had once been scattered all over the world now lived and worked within miles of one another.

With Drew's grandparents in town to care for him when they were gone, Dani and Chase were able to work in El Salvador or Honduras for a week twice a year together. Her mission work and her regular pediatric practice left Dani feeling deeply satisfied, knowing she was making a difference both in the U.S. and abroad. Chase stayed on at the mission another week on his own, which he said was the longest he could be away from his wife. Drew. It was the best of both worlds, as he liked to say, smiling and fulfilled when he returned home to his family.

Drew's pig puppet completely abandoned the cardboard "stage" and began chewing on Phil's leg. With a chuckle Chase stood and walked to stand behind Dani, wrapping his arms around her, his hands splayed across her big belly.

"That lizard's crazy in love with you, you know," he said next to her ear.

"Don't tell him, but I'm crazy in love with him,

too." She turned her face to his with a smile. He gave her a soft kiss, but his eyes were filled with mischief. And something else.

"He told me to ask you if he could lick you all over later. What do you say?"

She laughed and turned in his arms, her belly keeping them farther apart than she would have liked. "Tell him yes. I've always had a weakness for lizards."

He lowered his mouth to hers for a long, slow kiss and his lips were a far, far cry from any lizard's. Soft, warm, and, oh, so delicious, they tasted of all he'd given her.

Which was everything.

* * * * *